Unburied Fables

Printed in the United States of America

First Printing, 2016

ISBN-13: 978-1539302117
ISBN-10: 1539302113

Creative Aces Publishing
www.CreativeAcesPublishing.com

your story continues;

Table of Contents

Handsome and the Beast
by Laure Nepenthes

This story is based on "Beauty and the Beast," written more or less as we know it by French novelist Gabrielle-Suzanne Barbot de Villeneuve and adapted many times since.

Once upon a time, a long time ago, lived a couple of hard-working merchants. They had four children, two daughters and two sons. They were all well-read, gentle, and handsome.

The youngest was the most remarkable of them all. People admired him so much that they took to call him "little Handsome" and as he grew older, he still went by that name.

Handsome was a kind soul, with a love for all things that lived and grew. He spent his days studying the wonders of nature, with a particular fondness for flowers. He also read a great deal of poetry, philosophy, history, and tales from foreign lands.

Truth be told, there was little else he liked more than a quiet evening with a good book. He would always shy away from dances, especially after he came of age and people started to court him.

Noble girls in their best dresses or dashing gentlemen crowned with flowers and gems; Handsome would reject them all as politely as he could. To anyone who asked, he said that he wished never to marry. He was quite content with his books, his friends, and his family. He wished nothing more in the world than living among them for the rest of his life.

Fate might have heard him.

Suddenly, the merchants lost all their fortune, save for an old farm in the countryside. No more suitors came to the house. The family bid their servants goodbye before packing what they could not afford to sell.

They were saddened by the loss of comfort, money, and fame. Yet they were hard-working and honest, as many merchants are, so they resolved themselves to keep their chins up.

They needed that determination, for their new life was harsh. Every day, they would rise before the sun and work until night fell, tending to the fields or the house. It was the harshest on poor Handsome, who missed his books very much. But he also was the last to complain and the first to complete his chores, in the hope of having some time for himself.

The family had lived for about a year in such retirement when they heard that the last vessel carrying their trade had safely reached land.

The news turned the heads of children and parents alike. They would set to retrieve their goods at once, revive their business and move back to town!

Already they were dreaming of living in comfort again, of well-heated rooms and full wardrobes.

So confident they were that their situation would change for the better, the children asked for all sorts of presents from the port town: new clothes, new ribbons, all manners of trinkets and trifles.

Handsome himself only wished for new books, some ink and quills. However, encouraged by his siblings' eccentric requests, he asked for a rose instead.

"A rose, my dear son?"

"Yes, Father, if you please, the most beautiful you can find. I am so fond of them, yet none grow around these parts. I would very much like to see one again."

The merchants embraced their children and left that same day.

Unfortunately, a great fire burnt the town down before they arrived. Their ship was lost and so was their last chance at recovering their fortune.

With great chagrin, they went on their way back as poor as before.

They were not a day's walk from their house when they got lost in a deep forest.

They tried not to worry, but night fell and wolves howled in the distance. The merchants grew scared. They could survive a night out in the cold and the wind, but what could they do against wolves? As they looked for shelter among the woods, they thought less of themselves and more of their poor children. They lamented to themselves as they looked for their way out:

"What would happen to them, were we to die in this forest? Ah, they all have good heads on their shoulders. But what about Handsome? When his siblings start their own families, what will he do? How we wish he would not stay alone forever!"

Fate might have heard them.

The wind soon brought the scent of smoke and roasted meat. Walking in that direction, the merchants came across the ruins of a great castle in the heart of the woods.

Even in darkness, it looked imposing. Golden light poured from the open door, as if to invite them inside.

Yet all tired and frightened as they were, they also proved to be cautious and polite, as merchants are wont to be. They had heard of fairies living in those woods and did not wish to anger them.

"Hello! We are two poor merchants from the farm beyond the forest," they announced to the castle, "and we would be very much in your debt if we could spend the night here. Will you please allow us in?"

They stood on the threshold for a long while, calling and waiting, but nobody came to meet them. As the wind grew stronger and the howling closer, they resolved to enter, calling and apologising as they went.

Inside, they were surprised to see dinner set for two on a small table by a well-lit fireplace. The room used to be a great entrance hall, that much they could see, although it was now very dirty and cramped with debris of all kinds. Yet to the travel-weary merchants, it seemed as welcoming as the best inns they'd ever visited. They went and stood by the fire, warming their bones and waiting for the masters of the house.

They waited, and waited, and waited some more. Nobody came.

Each time the Father would move towards the table, the Mother would say, "We should wait a bit longer," and they would wait again, until the poor man was so hungry that he could stand it no more. He had gone through half a chicken by himself before his wife relented and joined him. They ate, they drank, and they thanked loudly and sincerely whatever kind fairy had prepared this meal for them.

After eating, they felt very sleepy, so they went and sat on an old couch in a corner of the room. They meant to wait for the masters of the house, but they had barely shed their coats when they fell into a deep slumber.

The sun was high in the sky when they woke up the next morning. For a moment, they did not know where they were, but as they got their bearings, they discovered that someone had dressed the table for two again, this time with enough for a hearty breakfast.

The merchants ate and drank merrily, for they had slept quite well and were feeling much better. Then they thanked the fairies once again and left the castle.

In the light of day, the ruins looked fantastic and grand, even in their state of abandonment.

"What a place," thought the merchants, "and what an amazing tale. Surely this will cheer up our children, even if we're not bringing back any of the gifts they asked."

Fate might have heard them.

As they went out, they saw the most delightful rosebush in the castle garden, blooming in vivid colors under the shining sun.

"We should take one for Handsome," suggested the Father, "At least one of us will have what he wished for."

"We have already been lucky enough," answered the Mother. "Let us walk away at once."

And walk away she did, but her husband stayed behind and reached for a branch. He plucked out one single rose, the prettiest he could see.

Immediately, a great roar rang out of the castle. The Mother went in hiding behind a tree; what she saw through the branches iced the blood in her very veins.

A frightful Beast had appeared at the door, all fur and scales, with antlers on their head and hooves instead of feet.

"How ungrateful you are!" growled the Beast to the Father. "Haven't I let you in my castle for the night?

Haven't I fed you, twice? And in return, you steal one of my roses, the one thing I value beyond anything in this world."

The Father fell to his knees and begged for forgiveness, but the Beast paid him no heed.

"This shall not go unpunished," they said, "and in repentance you shall stay here to serve me until the end of your days."

With another roar, they raised their arms to the skies. Thunder clapped. Suddenly, both Beast and Father were gone: only the rose remained, discarded on the ground. The Mother waited until she was sure that the Beast would not return and went to pick up the rose.

It was a wonderful flower, indeed. She had never seen its like before. It was not just one color, or two, but four: ebony, silver, snow white and purple, all at once.

She understood why the Beast treasured it so, but she did not think it was worth her husband's freedom. Still, she took it back home, as scant a consolation as could be.

In broad daylight, it did not take her much time to find her way back to the farm, where her children were waiting for her at the door. They immediately asked where their Father was, how did the business go, when would their Father return, and a dozen other questions.

For the longest time, the poor Mother could only cry and hold out that one rose, much to the siblings' confusion.

How they wept, when she told them the story of that night! They wept and pulled their hair and fell to their knees, save for Handsome, who remained silent, his eyes fixed on the rose.

"How can you be so cold, Handsome?" asked his siblings, "Aren't you sorry for our poor Father? Wasn't it you who wanted that flower which forced him into servitude?"

"Yes, it was me who asked for that rose," answered Handsome after a while, "and this is why I should be the one serving that Beast, not Father."

His mind was set.

They cried, they pleaded, they shouted. They told him, "The Beast will work you to death! You will not last a week! We should go and slay them instead!" But nothing shook his resolve.

His determination scared his siblings and his mother. They locked him in the bedroom while they devised a plan to gather warriors and free their Father.

Handsome wrote them a note instructing them to desist. Then he tucked the rose in his buttonhole, made a rope out of an old bedsheet and climbed out his window.

The forest was dark and deep, but Handsome's feet seemed to know the way. Soon enough he was at the castle gate, where he was surprised to see his own Father coming out to welcome him, dressed in a servant outfit.

The poor man seemed to have aged ten years, although barely a day had passed.

"Alas, my son! What are you doing here? Has your Mother not told you of my terrible punishment?"

"She has, Father. I wanted to thank you for getting that rose for me. It really is the most beautiful flower I have ever seen. Let me serve the Beast in your stead, so that I may see such wonder every day."

The Father tried to protest, since this was a lie and they both knew it, but at that moment the Beast appeared behind him. They looked even scarier than Handsome had expected, but he did not step back. He gave them his most polite bow.

"Is that true, child?" asked the Beast. "Do you wish to take your Father's place?"

"I do, my Liege," answered Handsome. "Please have mercy on an old man and let me serve you instead."

The Beast thought about this for a little while, his goat eyes going from Handsome to his father to Handsome again.

"A young servant is better than an old one," they decided, "Let it be so!"

With this, the Beast raised their arms. Thunder filled the sky. Handsome covered his eyes in fear. When he opened his eyes again, he was wearing the Beast's colors; black, grey, white, and green. He was standing on the other side of the gate, and his Father, now in his traveling clothes, was standing in Handsome's place.

They had little time to say their goodbyes. The Beast started walking back into the castle, and Handsome had to follow.

The rooms inside were not as filthy as Handsome had feared, although they were in a great state of chaos and decay. Beast and boy walked through endless

9

corridors. Each room they passed by still bore the trace of its past magnificence, old gold glimmering on the peeling walls.

"What do you wish me to do, my Liege?" asked Handsome after a great deal of walking.

"My name is not Liege, or Master, or anything so grand," answered the Beast. "A Beast is what I am and such is my name. What is yours, child?"

"I am called Handsome, Beast. People have been calling me so since I was very little."

"Have they, now? Well, Handsome, today you will sweep the floors of all my rooms. You will tell me which one is your favourite tonight."

The Beast left him with his task and a broom that had seen better days.

Handsome did not think for one second that he could complete his work on time. He also wished he had a shovel or a hammer instead of a broom. There were many broken pieces of furniture and stones scattered all over the castle. A broom would not be enough to clear it all.

But he was determined and used to toil after a year on the farm, so he set to work anyway. He swept his way through libraries, kitchens, ballrooms, bathrooms, stairways, bedrooms; down to the lowest cellars and up to the conservatory on the highest floor.

When sun set, he was still working. He felt exhausted, but he was far from being done. Thinking he would have to stop soon and look for a light, he took the time to yawn and rub his eyes.

Thunder boomed as he did, and when he opened them again, he was standing in the entrance hall. A great fire was burning in the fireplace and dinner for one was set on the little table.

The Beast was sitting in a large armchair close to the fire, their goat eyes half-closed in thought.

"Sit down and eat," they said after a long silence. "Then tell me which room is your favorite."

Handsome thanked them and did as he was told. He had not realised how famished he was and felt a great delight at eating. However, he grew uneasy when he finished his plate and realised that he had not given the Beast's question any thought.

"I like all your rooms, Beast," said he when his plate was empty, "for although there are many of them, and they are all needing a lot of work, I can tell that they were all beautiful and that they all served a purpose."

The Beast did not move or say a word. Handsome wondered if they had expected a more precise answer, so he added: "I think the conservatory is the one I liked best. If restored, one could tend to flowers, stargaze, or read, all in natural light. It surely sounds very pleasing."

The Beast did not answer. Their eyes were now fully closed.

Handsome thought they might have fallen asleep, so he excused himself from the table as softly as he could and went to sleep on the old couch in the corner of the room.

That night, he dreamt that he walked through the conservatory as it must once have been: full of colors and

11

peaceful silence, stars shining bright above the glass ceiling.

Someone was reading on a lounge chair. Handsome tried to get close, but he could not see their face. A door opened to the side, letting faint rumors of music and laughter flow into the room.

"Won't you come to the ball, my precious child?" asked a richly-dressed woman.

Handsome could not hear the reader's voice, but he knew their answer in his heart: "I'd rather read my book, Mother."

"But my dearest sweetheart," said the woman, "so many young men and women are here to meet you. Why must you refuse their courtship?"

All turned to black before Handsome could know what the reader would answer to this. Another woman's voice echoed in the darkness. She said: "There once was a child who did not wish to be courted. All day, they remained in a world of fantasy and dreams in order to escape their parents' pressure."

When Handsome woke up, a plentiful breakfast was waiting for him on the little table, along with a note from the Beast: "Today, you are to sort all the books in my library. You will tell me which one is your favorite tonight."

Handsome sighed deeply. Another impossible task! And what a queer dream, too. As he ate and started to work, his mind kept wandering back to the mysterious reader. Who were they? What book were they reading?

No answer came to him, and soon the task at hand required all his attention. It was much harder than he had imagined: Handsome loved books so much that, more than once, he caught himself reading instead of sorting them as the Beast had asked.

Each seemed even more interesting than the last one. They covered a wide range of topics, from ancient history to music, travel journals and mathematics.

Handsome worked and read all day. Whenever he was hungry, thunder would roll, and food would appear before him. Each time, Handsome took great care to thank the Beast loudly and genuinely for feeding him. He thought that they were in league with some fairies, for he had read many tales when he was younger; but he had no time or strength to devote to that line of thought, because he still had so much work to do.

He worked until the sun set, and then some more; as he paused to rub his eyes once, thunder cracked and he found himself in the entrance hall. The Beast was sitting in their armchair and dinner for one was set on the little table.

"Won't you eat with me, Beast?" asked Handsome as he sat in front of his plate. Surely that was not his place to ask, but he was raised a free man and thus was not accustomed to acting like a servant. He also thought that the Beast might get a little lonely, always on their own in such a big castle.

"I already have, Handsome," answered the Beast, "Now tell me, which book of mine was your favorite?"

"I had not the time to sort them all, I'm afraid," said Handsome. This was no lie, but he had not given the question any thought either. "But they all look so interesting. It is too hard to choose, but maybe I like the travel stories the best, with all their maps and watercolors."

Like the night before, the Beast closed their eyes and remained silent. Handsome ate his meal, excused himself from the table in a whisper and went to sleep on the old couch.

He had a feeling that he might dream again that night—and he did. He was in the castle library, all well-lit, clean, and full of books. The reader from the previous night was there as well, peering over a map. Handsome could not see their face, but he had an idea of who they might be.

A servant entered and bowed deeply.

"Their Highness' Father is calling for them. He is, if I may, quite angry."

Once again, Handsome could not hear the reader's voice, but he knew their answer in his heart: "He wishes for me to choose a spouse. I have refused to marry many times, and I shall not change my mind. Tell him I will not go."

The scene turned black, as it had done the night before, and the same voice echoed in the dark: "The child's parents grew restless, but no matter the questioning, cajoling, or prodding, the child would not relent."

Handsome woke up to breakfast on the table and another note from the Beast: "Today, you will count the trees in the garden. You will tell me which one you prefer tonight."

Now, Handsome was no fool: twice he had been given an impossible task and a question, but twice only the question had mattered, and twice he had dreamt of his answer on the following night.

Third time makes the charm, as they said. Handsome resolved to find his favourite tree instead of working himself to exhaustion as he had done on the two previous days.

He walked through the garden feeling quite confident, but soon his hopes dwindled. The garden was greatly overgrown and home to too many trees. There were oak, birch, pine, fir, and many more, among which were a great deal he had never heard or read about before. Every time Handsome thought he'd found the one, another would appear that he would like even more. But he knew that there could only be one correct answer, and so he kept on searching.

As on the two previous days, whenever he felt hungry or thirsty, thunder crashed and food or water appeared out of thin air. And as soon as he rubbed his eyes after sunset, he was back in the entrance hall with his dinner ready for him and the Beast sitting by the fireplace.

"Will you come and eat with me, Beast?" asked Handsome as he sat down.

"I already have, Handsome, but I might sit with you tomorrow," answered the Beast, "Now, tell me, what's your favourite tree in my garden?"

"I am very sorry, Beast, but I did not have quite the time. You have more beautiful trees than I have ever imagined could exist. My parents always say that sleep brings good counsel: if you allow me, I will give you my answer by morning."

The Beast scoffed. Handsome feared he had irritated them, but they said nothing and closed their eyes. He hurried himself to eat and quickly went to sleep.

As he had expected, that night he dreamt of the castle garden, well-cared for and in full bloom.

The reader was there once again, with their face still invisible to Handsome. That mattered little: he knew who they were. In the dream, they sat beneath a cherry tree, braiding roses into a flower crown. These were plain yellow roses, not the four-colored ones that grew around the castle. A woman was standing next to them, lavishly clad in pearls and feathers, under a cape that shone with all the colors of the rainbow.

"Your Highness," she said. Handsome recognised the mysterious voice he had heard the nights before. "I am the Queen of Fairies. Your parents demand I curse you. They do not understand your heart's desire and see you as a Beast. I cannot refuse them: they see you as a Beast and thus a Beast you will be. But there is, I am sure, something I could offer to you in exchange?"

Handsome could not hear the Beast's voice but he knew their words in his heart: "I care not to be a Beast, nor do I wish to make a bargain with a Fairy. But since I don't have any choice, I want enough of your magic to enjoy my books and my castle for as long as I wish. Oh, and I wish to be a Beast strong enough to go and see the most wonderful flowers of this world."

The Fairy nodded and smiled. "Do not worry, Beast: the most beautiful roses will soon grow all around your castle."

Then she raised her hands. Thunder cracked. All faded to black.

The Fairy's voice echoed in Handsome's dream: "You are a gentle soul, child. Take caution of this tale. Sometimes there is more goodness in the hearts of Beasts than in those of people."

Before he could answer, he was awoken.

"Beast!" he cried as he jumped from the old couch, "Beast, where are you? I know which tree is my favorite!"

"I hear you, Handsome," the Beast drawled, standing by one of the great windows in the hall. "Do tell me."

"It's the great cherry tree underneath which the Fairy cursed you, isn't it?"

"Yes," answered the Beast softly. "Yes, it is."

Silence fell between the boy and the Beast; he had so many questions to ask, he did not even know where to begin.

"You've worked hard, Handsome," spoke the Beast again, "and now your reward has come. Your siblings are here. They have come with knives and pitchforks. Villagers march with them. They intend to strike me down and free you from my service. This is not bad thinking: my fur and my antlers will fetch a good price, and you can go back to a life of comfort in the city."

With those words, the Beast walked out of the door, determined to meet their end.

"Halt, halt, pray stop at once!" cried Handsome as he ran after them, "Do not harm them! I beg of you all, do not harm each other!"

His parents and siblings, who were not sure if they would ever see him again, brought him into their embrace.

"Oh, Handsome! We are so glad to see you well. Let us slay this foul Beast and return home."

"They are no Beast!" said Handsome. "Well, they are, but they are not bad. They treated me well and I wish to stay with them. Go home before anyone gets hurt."

For a while, it was all confusion and shouting, everyone trying to speak over everyone else. Handsome tried to convince one or the other of his relatives, but nobody was listening to him. More than once he had to throw himself between the Beast and the pitchforks.

It took a mighty roar from the Beast to calm everyone down.

"Why are you doing this, Handsome?" they asked.

"I have never wished to marry either," explained Handsome, "and I have always liked books better than dances. By that reasoning, I am myself a little of a Beast, but my parents have been more understanding than yours. I think you have a kind heart, Beast, and we share the same tastes. Allow me to go as I please, treat me as your equal; I will be your friend and you will be mine. No blood will be shed and everyone will be happy. Would that not be nice, Beast?"

"Yes," answered the Beast after a long while. "That would be very nice, indeed." Then, with their mighty voice, they called: "Queen of the Fairies!"

Thunder shook the sky and the Fairy Queen was among them.

"Dear Queen," said the Beast as they bowed, "I wish to strike a bargain with you. I will give you all the roses in my garden that have bloomed this year if you give me enough of your magic to ensure Handsome a comfortable stay in my castle."

The Fairy laughed, but did not say a word. She raised her hand, but instead of thunder, her laughter grew, and grew, and grew. It grew until it rang in the ears of everyone, like water cascading from a torrent. Suddenly, gone were the flowers on the rosebush and the Queen in her beautiful dress. Handsome was wearing his favourite clothes instead of the servant outfit and the castle had been restored to its former glory. Everything was marble and gold as far as the eye could see. The windows had glass again, and the ceiling was covered in colourful tiles.

"Now, be happy, children," sang the Queen's voice from the sky, "and never let anyone doubt the goodness of your hearts."

No one could stand against Handsome's honest offer of friendship, especially not one blessed by the Queen of Fairies. Pitchforks were brought down and knives were sheathed. The Beast did their best to show themselves polite and agreeable. They showed their guests the bedrooms and their comfortable beds, the well-polished furniture in the reception halls, the full pantries in the kitchens and the shiny bathtub in the bathroom.

Then, after making him promise that he would visit soon, his family left Handsome with the Beast, but not without threatening them to "take care of him...or else!"

Thus started a new life for Handsome and the Beast, as equals and in good friendship. Food did not appear whenever they were hungry anymore, but the Beast was a good hunter and Handsome had learned how to grow vegetables at the farm. They would have dinner together every night, discussing the new books they had read or planning their next journey.

In time, they made other friends, Beasts and humans alike. They visited faraway lands and discovered many new flowers. Before long, they had settled in happiness, unmarried but not unloved, and thus they stayed until the end of their days.

The Grateful Princess
by Rachel Sharp

This story is based on the Estonian fairy tale "The Grateful Prince." Though the origin is a subject of some mystery, a version appeared in Andrew Lang's <u>The Violet Fairy Book</u>, published in 1901.

In all of time and space, there is a law that holds true. It governs the smallest part of homemaking as well as the largest affairs of the heart. Most cultures have a common saying for it. Sometimes it gets buried in fine print. The law, of course, is *buyer beware*.

Unfortunately, the kingdom of Armastus had no such saying.

This may be why the king was so foolish.

Lost in the woods with only his horse and a water skin, he was starting to get desperate. The road was long gone. Though his stewards worried about his riding alone so far from the village, he had ignored them. He may be an old man, but he refused to be considered weak. These woods should be as familiar to him as his own castle.

Possibly his mind was going.

On the third day, the king was leading his horse down to an unfamiliar stream when a stranger appeared before him. Strange was indeed the word: A man older than himself, small and twisted yet surprisingly fine of feature, stepped from the trees and hailed him. The king was exhausted. He demanded that the stranger give him direction back to the castle.

The stranger offered him a deal.

The king rarely had to make any compromise, but this time he seemed to have no choice. He agreed. The stranger led him back to the road, and the king was on his way.

What a strange request, the king thought. *Direction in exchange for the first thing to emerge from my castle upon my arrival. It could be anything. It could be the midden cart.* Secretly, he feared that his beloved hunting dog would be loose and would run to him. The loss of the dog would pain him.

It never occurred to him that it would be his child.

When the king was greeted at the gate by the face of his infant daughter, carried in the arms of a nurse, his distress was inexplicable to those around him. He had been tricked. The stranger somehow knew that this would happen. Now that he was in his own castle, with food, water, and clean clothes in front of him, he raged against the deal he had made. The stranger had taken him for a fool. The bargain was unfair and could not possibly be enforced. And yet, the king had to appear a man of his word.

He told the truth to no one.

That night, he ordered that his daughter be switched for a peasant child in the village. He explained to the steward who carried out this task that it was to bar against threats to the royal line.

When the stranger came to claim his prize, the king handed over the peasant child. He announced to his subjects, as he had said to the steward before, that the child was entrusted to another's care to bar against threats to the royal line.

It would be safe.

And safe in far distant houses, both children grew into young women, having never known anything else.

)

"I can't be a princess. That's absurd!" Tuline cried, leaping from her chair. Her parents sat across from her, frozen in front of their simple meal.

"I'm sorry, Tuline," her mother said, shrinking into her seat. "It was for your safety. The king himself sent a message asking this of us, and you're nearly of age. Soon someone will come to reclaim you, and then we will learn what became of our own daughter. The—"

"You *traded* me?" Tuline paced across the wooden floor, bumping into the furniture and gesturing wildly. "Not only am I a, a *princess* raised to feed goats and make butter, but you *traded* me for *your own child*?"

"Yes," her father said, trying to use his voice to restore order and calm.

"And you don't know what happened to your daughter?"

"No."

Tuline raised her hands to the ceiling as if asking for an answer, but then shook her head and dropped them to her hips.

"Well," she said. "That won't do at all."

Tuline fled the house against her parents' protests and ran straight to the castle, her gangly legs finally doing her some good. A guard stopped her at the gate.

"I am the princess, I have returned home, and you will let me through," Tuline told them, adopting the same tone that had so cowed her parents. In the guard's moment of hesitation, she blew by him and raced to the servant's quarters, which she located by finding the plainest hallway and bursting through the plainest door.

People in various stages of dress looked up at her in alarm.

"Who took the princess to a peasant's home sixteen summers ago?" Tuline demanded.

There were whispers.

Such a thing never happened.

She is a wild woman.
What is she doing here?

But finally, Tuline heard a sigh from a simple bed in the back of the hall, and a man in a steward's green-trimmed uniform came forward.

"I did this thing," he said. "My name is Usal, and in my prime I was the king's most trusted steward."

"Where is the peasant child now?" Tuline asked him.

"Only the king knows," said Usal.

Tuline went to the doors of throne room and shouted until the king could not ignore her.

He ordered everyone else away.

He told her everything.

It wasn't hard for Tuline to get lost in the woods. She'd never been this far from home before. The king had tried to convince her not to go, but in the end, he gave her a cloak and a bag full of traveling supplies, wishing her well. Tuline looked into his face and wondered if he hoped for his own redemption by her action.

She had also run back to her home for a sack of lavender seeds that her mother kept in the garden shed. The protests of her parents went unheeded. Wandering through the woods, she dropped seeds behind her and tried her hardest to look desperate.

By the third day, looking desperate was no longer difficult. Her food had run out, and even her strong legs were starting to fail her. The cloak from the king was covered in dirt and burrs. As Tuline staggered to a stream to fill her water skin, the stranger finally appeared from behind a large oak.

"You are deep in the woods," the stranger said to her. "Have you lost the road?"

Tuline put on her saddest face. "Oh, sir! I was traveling home to plant lavender on my father's grave when the sun set and I strayed! I can not find my way!"

The stranger put a hand to his heart. "Waylaid on such an errand. What an awful thing. I can show you the road, but I'm afraid my lot in life is not so good that I can pass up asking something in return. If you will come to my farm and finish the work that so overwhelms me, I will guide you home."

"Oh, thank you!" Tuline cried, curtsying as she imagined a princess would. Embarking on a quest and sorting out a crisis of identity at the same time might cause her some fumbling, but she could always learn how to be a princess when she had less important things to do.

The stranger led her away, and Tuline followed, dropping lavender seeds the whole way.

The stranger, who called himself Jube, led Tuline through caverns to a secret valley hemmed in by mountains. There before her was a sprawling farm. Something here was wrong. It seemed that, out of the corner of her eye, she would catch a horse moving with impossible speed, or a cow laying down on a cloud...but when she looked, nothing was out of the ordinary.

Jube gave her an empty kennel to sleep in. It smelled of sulfur rather than dog, and strange scrabbling sounds came through the wall, but she was exhausted. She slept soundly under her cloak.

The next day, Jube called her to serve breakfast. Tuline found that there were settings for two people at the table, and as she shoveled potatoes onto the second plate, a young woman entered the room. Smaller than Tuline herself, this woman had the black hair and brown eyes of Tuline's mother. Her clothing was fine, but her manner was distressed. *My parents' true daughter*, Tuline thought. *She's beautiful. Her hair looks so soft. I hope she thinks I'm beautiful, too.*

Tuline shook her head to clear it, fairly certain that princesses didn't think such things. Besides, it seemed unlikely that the gentle newcomer would ever find her striking. Tuline was all awkward limbs and callouses. This peasant girl looked more like a princess than she ever would.

"This is my daughter, Lind," Jube said. "You will not speak to her. You may have the scraps when we are done."

Tuline tried to disobey and tell the girl her name, but found that she could not. Jube had some kind of control over her, some dark magic that kept her throat from moving to make words. She thought to shout, to protest Jube's theft of her voice, but decided to be cautious.

If he has that kind of power, she thought, *coming here may have been a terrible mistake.*

After breakfast, she devoured the scraps left behind. It seemed to her that Lind had barely touched her meal, leaving more for Tuline. Maybe the beautiful girl liked her after all.

Jube returned to the kitchen with a scythe. "My task for you," he said, "is to clean out the white horse's stall and feed the creature fresh hay until he will eat no more. Come to me when you are done."

Tuline was delighted. She was a farm girl, after all. Cleaning a stall and feeding a horse was easier than skipping stones. She nodded to Jube and took the scythe, practically prancing on her way to cut some fresh grasses. She cut down a mountainous pile of hay with her long, swinging arms before laying it out for the white horse. When she finished mucking out the stable, she found that all of the hay was gone and the horse was looking at her impatiently. She cut more hay, and then more, but still the beast ate every bit. By the time she returned with a ninth armload of hay, the stall needed cleaning again.

"Pssst."

Tuline looked around. Lind's brown eyes were looking at her over the edge of the stall. Tuline continued shoveling but watched the girl to show that she was listening.

"That is no earthly horse. He will eat forever unless you bind his mouth with woven grasses. Here." Lind flung a grass rope over the edge. Tuline caught it. When she looked back up, Lind had vanished. Tuline, figuring that the stunning stranger knew more about this odd farm than she herself, tied the rope around the horse's mouth and brought in another armload of hay.

The horse snorted, but did not eat. Tuline returned to the house.

Jube looked up from a worn book, eyeing her suspiciously. "The horse has had his fill?"

"You can see for yourself. There is hay untouched in his stall." Tuline was happy to find that her voice was lost only with Lind, and that to Jube, she could still speak her mind.

"Good, yes," said Jube. "I also need the goat milked. I need every last drop."

Tuline nodded again and headed for the barn, wondering what the difficulty would be this time.

In the barn, she found a white goat, a bucket, and a three-legged stool. Trying to milk the goat, she found that no matter what she did, the animal gave only one drop of milk at a time. She sighed and put her head in her hands. This would take a season.

Again, she heard "Psssst."

Lind was passing by the barn, trying not to look like she had paused.

Tuline gave her a helpless look.

"You have to threaten her or she won't give milk," Lind said. Then she scurried on her way.

Tuline looked around the barn, finally settling on pair of tongs hanging by the door. She heated them in the fire of the little forge and waved them in front of the goat. "If you don't give me milk when I squeeze with my hands, I'll have to use these instead," she said, giving the goat her haughtiest stare. The goat kicked over the milking stool in protest, but then lowered its head and let Tuline milk it in peace. She returned to the house with a brimming bucket.

This time, Jube was livid. He snatched the milk away before regaining his composure.

"Wonderful!" he said, setting the milk down. "There's only one more thing I need, and then I will get you to the road. In the barn is a white calf. Bring him to the farthest pasture."

Tuline walked away, expecting the calf to be a hundred hands tall and made of stone.

Instead, she found the smallest calf she had ever seen, hidden in the farthest stall. Tuline grabbed a rope from the wall and reached for the calf, but her hand passed right through. Confused, she tried again. The calf showed no reaction as she walked around and finally straight through it. It seemed to glow. Tuline thought her eyes must be playing tricks.

"Pssst."

Tuline turned gratefully towards the source of the sound. This time, Lind was trying to look occupied at a butter churn.

"The calf is made of purest light," she said. "To lead it, you must steady your hand and use only the most delicate silk."

Tuline dropped the rope and waved her empty hands. She had no silk. Lind realized the problem and laughed. "Come, take a thread from my dress. Try to be quick. It mustn't look like I'm helping you, if that beast Jube is watching."

After a moment's hesitation, Tuline snuck around behind the other girl and plucked a single long thread from her collar, accidentally brushing the side of Lind's neck. Tuline felt her face flush. She had so many questions. Why was Lind helping her? What did Jube really want from her? Why were the animals here so strange? Why did she herself have such strong feelings for Lind, who was both a girl and a commoner?

She tried to sigh, but her throat wouldn't let her. When last the sun set, she had been a girl who made the best goat butter in the village. Now she was a princess, in love with a woman, in a strange valley where horses had bottomless stomachs and cows were made of pure light.

Creeping back to the calf's stall, she tried to tie the silk around its neck. Her hands shook. The silk fell through.

Calm, she told herself. *Steady hands. I am the same person I was before, and outside of this valley, the world is still the same world.*

Finally, the silk lay gently across the calf's neck. She tied a tiny knot and led it outside to the farthest pasture.

When she returned to the house, Jube was standing at the window. He stared at the calf in the field.

"Well done!" he cried, but his face was tight. His smile was as thin as the silk thread. "I will take you to the road when the sun rises! For tonight, we should both rest."

Tuline nodded, thinking of nothing she could say to this bizarre monster that Lind so disliked, and retreated to her kennel.

Lind came to her in the night, slipping in quietly while Tuline slept under her cloak. Lind's gentle touch on her arm startled Tuline into wakefulness.

"We must leave tonight," Lind said. "Jube doesn't mean to take you home. He has powers, *wrongful* powers. He forces lost travelers to stay until he turns them into animals. Someday he will grow tired of me and I, too, will be made a calf or a mare! I tried many times to run, once I learned of the world outside the valley, but he sends the horrible goblins from these very kennels after me, and each time I am caught. If we run together, we may be able to make an escape!"

For the hundredth time, Tuline wished she could speak to Lind.

The young woman pulled a crystal from her pocket. It glowed faintly in the dark of the kennel. "Jube mines these from the tunnels that lead out of the valley. They are the source of his strange power. The last time I ran, I pulled this one from the ground before I was caught and hid it well. With this magic, we may be able to escape him."

Tuline put her hand on Lind's, touching the crystal. She felt as if an unseen rope had been eased from her throat and cried out in surprise.

"Ah! I can speak to you!"

Lind smiled and lifted the crystal. "Magic."

Tuline held her hand a little tighter.

"We should run."

When Jube awoke, he searched and searched for Lind and Tuline, but finally he realized the truth. They had gone. He howled and stomped at their defiance.

Certain that he could get them back, he released all the goblins from his kennels to give chase, and they echoed his howl through the caverns, heading for the world outside.

Exiting the caves into the bright sunlight, Tuline let go of Lind's hand and pointed. A path of purple led away into the woods. "The lavender seeds I dropped! They've flowered! How long have I been gone?"

Lind shook her head. "Jube's magic. Time is different in the valley. I have long suspected that Jube sped and halted my aging as it suited him. The lavender path is a great good for us. We must hurry."

But as Tuline and Lind raced along the path of flowers, they heard the scrabbling and howling of goblins behind them.

"They'll catch us!" Lind shouted, trying to force her stride further and faster. Her legs were not as long as Tuline's.

"No, they won't," said Tuline. She grabbed Lind's hand again, the crystal between their fingers, and wished as hard as she could for them to be swift. She closed her eyes and felt her feet disappear beneath her, then her whole body fading away. She became the wind blowing through the lavender, and felt within herself the presence of Lind, transformed into a sparrow by the crystal she carried in her beak. Together they swept through the forest. The goblins could never catch them now.

When they arrived at the end of the lavender path, the village lay before them. Lind used the crystal to restore their true forms. Then she turned to Tuline.

Despite their glorious escape, Lind's face was still filled with fear.

"You must go home," she said.

"I do not know where my home is," Tuline said. "I learned just before I came for you that I am the princess, and that you were switched for me when we were young so that Jube would take you instead. The home I thought I had is truly yours. The castle is no home for me, either."

Tuline looked down at her boots. "It seems more fitting that you should be the princess, for you are lovely and poised, and I am all over callouses and tend to knock things down."

Lind reached out and laid a delicate hand on Tuline's cheek. "You are strong and brave as well as lovely. You will be a powerful princess and work for the good of the people, for you know the people in your bones. I only wish I could stay with you. But Jube will never stop hunting me. I must go."

Tuline reached for her, but before anything more could be said, Lind used the crystal to transform herself back into a sparrow and flew away once more with the stone in her beak. Tuline watched her go, feeling as if she had bested the monsters of the valley and yet still, somehow, lost everything.

In time, she returned to the castle.

Upon her arrival, a steward dressed in black informed her that the old king had passed while she was away. Then he bowed to her deeply. She was the only survivor of the royal line. The king, ridden by guilt, had confessed to everything on his deathbed. Tuline was now the queen of Armastus.

Though servants fussed around her, bringing her fine clothes and food and drawing her more hot baths than she could stand, the young queen had other things on her mind. She called for Usal, the steward who had taken her from the castle as a child, and told him to gather the commoners of the village for a royal decree.

She told them everything, so that her entire kingdom would know that she started her dealings with them fairly and honestly, and knew to beware of the stranger in the woods.

Then she asked them for their help.

"Lind is lost to me," she said, fidgeting with the lace on her itchy, extravagant gown. "She feared that her presence would endanger me, but now that I am queen, she can come to live in the castle where she will be safe. Please help me find her. I will offer any reward you ask."

She thought for a moment.

"Excepting the kingdom or my first born," Tuline said. "I have fallen in love with Lind, and will have no first born. If she is returned to me, we will take the orphans of the village into our care instead, and one of them shall inherit the kingdom."

Then she turned and attempted a stately retreat. She avoided tripping on her dress only because she insisted on wearing her sturdy farm boots underneath, which kept her footsteps strong.

In the weeks that followed, Tuline learned to be queen. Her people learned to love her, for she was generous and fair. She understood the trials and trivialities of common life. By day, she looked after her kingdom. By night, she worried about Lind.

Finally, the people she had thought of as her parents came to the castle. The only mother Tuline had ever known held a sparrow in her hands.

"She flew in through the window of our cottage, my queen," the woman said. "Though I long to meet the woman who might have been my daughter, I believe she was searching for you."

Tuline gently reached out and took the bird from her with hands that were still calloused from work in the castle vegetable gardens. The sparrow still held a tiny crystal in her beak. Tuline whispered to the bird.

"Lind. You will be safe here. All of the kingdom will throw stones at Jube if he ever shows himself again. I love you. I wish to share my kingdom with you." Tuline started to cry. "I give everything I have for my people, and your love is the one thing I wish for myself."

The sparrow pressed against her hand, but did not change back into a woman.

Her mother put a hand on Tuline's shoulder. "Lind is fearful," she said. "Give her time."

Tuline nodded.

That night, she took a large birdcage from the palace stores and carried it to the forge herself, ordering that the doors be welded open so that Lind would always be free. She placed the cage in a room of its own, and left that door open, too. Every day, Tuline visited Lind, hoping that someday the sparrow would transform back into her beloved.

In time, the sparrow did just that, and they lived happily ever after.

Odd
by Amy Michelle

A retelling of "Rumpelstiltskin," a fairy tale first recorded by the Brothers Grimm but suspected to be much older in origin.

As the story goes, a baker's daughter lived in a faraway kingdom. Known as Sofia, she was her father's pride and joy, and he loved her with all his heart. Unfortunately for her, he showed his love by boasting about everything she did. He would tell anyone who listened about her beauty and her many talents, both real and imagined. If he didn't brag about her, he bragged about his status as one of the best bakers in the land. More often than not, his boasts only brought them trouble.

"My bread will not mold!" he once told a passing gentleman. When the man returned to complain that the dozens of loaves he'd purchased had molded, it fell on Sofia to apologize and find a solution.

"I can provide five hundred cakes for your party tomorrow!" he promised a lord. When he and Sofia could only deliver a fraction of the dessert, it again fell on Sofia to keep the lord from arresting her father.

"My daughter is the most beautiful girl in the land! Not even the princess can compare to her beauty and grace!" Sofia had countless young people arrive at the bakery to see her, interrupting her work and rarely buying anything.

It was reasonable, then, that she did not want her father to go to the palace and meet with the king. All the bakers in the land had been invited by his majesty, who needed a new Royal Baker, to present their finest breads and pastries for him to judge. Whoever the king chose would be solely responsible for the royal bakery on a daily basis, as well as cakes and assorted baked goods for royal balls. Sofia knew it would be a nightmare.

"Don't go," she said, not for the first time, while her father finished packing their cart with cakes, pies, and loaves of bread.

He closed the back of the cart and gave her a patient smile. "I can't very well decline an invitation from the crown," he said. "Besides, all our hard work would go to waste."

She sighed heavily. "If you're set on going, at least be honest. Don't oversell what we can do."

"I would never!"

Sofia glowered, but all her father did was grin.

"I mean it," she said.

Her father laughed and pulled himself into the seat of the cart. "Fine," he said. He clicked the reigns and the cart lurched forward, her father whistling merrily from the front.

"And leave me out of it all!"

Her father's laughter drifted back and Sofia felt her stomach sink. Something was going to go wrong. She just knew it.

His return did not disappoint.

"You did *what*?"

Her father had the grace to look sheepish while Sofia could only gape at him. "I was only thinking of your future…"

"My future!?" Sofia laughed harshly. "You lied to the king because you thought it would help my *future*? How am I supposed to turn straw into gold?"

"His majesty said you could marry his son once the feat is complete…or his daughter, whoever you prefer."

Sofia shook her head, fighting back tears. "I'm not interested in the prince *or* the princess," she said. "You know I don't feel attraction like that."

"I just—"

"Stop. Don't try to come up with an excuse. I'll…I'll figure something out. I always do."

A knock at the front door interrupted their argument. A young soldier entered before being invited and glanced at Sofia's father. "Is she ready?" they asked.

"I'm ready," Sofia replied before her father had a chance. She followed them out the door before her father could come up with any other defense for his actions, her head held high. The soldier helped Sofia into a waiting carriage and climbed in after her. The two sat in silence as the carriage took off towards the palace.

The soldier glanced once or twice at Sofia during the trip before steeling their nerve to ask, "Is it true? You can spin straw into gold?"

Sofia met the young person's eyes and gave a wry smile. "I guess we'll find out," she replied. "What happens if I can't?"

The soldier's curious gaze turned to pity and they didn't answer, confirming Sofia's suspicions. They finished their journey in silence.

Sofia barely paid attention to the ornate beauty surrounding her as they arrived at the palace. She stayed focused on how she could get out of this mess as the soldier led her to the throne room. Only when she became aware of the king, sitting on a raised dais looking down on her, did she drop into a low curtsey. "Your majesty."

"Ah, you must be the baker's daughter!" The king stood from his throne and approached her, sizing her up as he did. "I'm very excited to meet you."

"Yes, about that, your majesty—"

"Now, now," he patted her arm sympathetically. "No need to thank me. I know it's an honor to serve your king."

"Yes, your majesty, quite the honor, but—"

"Your father was quite adamant about your talents. I'm sure you will not disappoint." He placed a firm hand on her arm to guide her out of the throne room, through a series of hallways. "Your contributions to the kingdom will go far. We will have more trading power, the ability to build our army and navy, put people to work. The impact it will have! Everyone will be affected, from the highest lord to the common stable boy; it is truly amazing what good gold can do. And to have you to produce it for us! It makes you a worthy bride for my son or daughter."

"I don't...your majesty, I don't want to marry a royal child."

"Noble of you; though I can think of no finer reward for your service."

Sofia clenched her fist at her side. "Your children are not just something to reward a job well done. I'm sure they are marvelous people, but I don't see the appeal of a relationship."

The king glanced at her as they stopped outside a plain wooden door. "Regardless. If you succeed, you will be a queen."

"Your majesty...my father...my father tends to exaggerate. He wasn't exactly..."

The king's look grew dark. "I'm sure your father knows better than to lie to a king," he said. "If he did lie, and you can't turn this straw into gold, that would be considered treason. I don't know if you're aware, but the penalty for treason is death. And I'm sure neither of us would want to see it come to that."

He reached into his pocket and withdrew a key, unlocking the door in front of them. He steered her into the room, filled floor to ceiling with straw. "I expect this room to be filled with gold when I return in the morning. If it isn't, well..."

The threat hung between them. Sofia felt tears in her eyes. The king turned abruptly and shut the door behind him.

Once the king left, Sofia took a deep breath, wiped her eyes, and surveyed her surroundings. She did a lap around the room and found nothing but a fireplace, spinning wheel, and piles and piles of straw. Not even a blanket or window. She tried the door, even though she knew what she would find. Locked. With nothing else to do, she sat down at the spinning wheel and gave it a whirl. She didn't even know how to use one, never mind use it to turn straw into gold. She groaned and covered her face with her hands, torn between crying and raging. If she didn't turn the straw into gold, she and her father would be arrested for treason. She had no doubt that the king would use her father as incentive to make her try again. After all, if "rewarding" her with his children didn't motivate her, losing her family should. She didn't want to think about what would happen if she still failed.

"Quite the pickle you've found yourself in," came a melodious voice from the top of one of the piles of straw. "Judging that you haven't started spinning, I'm supposing you can't."

Sofia's head shot up. "Who are you?" she asked. "How did you get in here?"

"Now, now. Can't go giving all my secrets away. All that matters is, I know you need me." Sofia could only stare at the person before her, completely different from her in every way. Where Sofia's hair fell down her back in a dark sheet, the stranger's curled in every direction around their head. Her skin appeared bronze in the firelight and the stranger's was so dark, it seemed to drink light in. The brightest thing about the stranger was their eyes, shining clear and blue from a mischievous round face. Sofia's own brown eyes seemed ordinary in comparison.

"You're right," Sofia said slowly, "I do need you. But why would you help me?"

The stranger shrugged. "Maybe you seem like you deserve it. Maybe I have a thing for subverting authority. The important thing is, I'm here, and I expect more gratitude."

"Thank you," Sofia said quickly, dropping her eyes. She wasn't going to look too closely at this gift the universe had given her. "But what can I do—"

"That necklace is quite nice."

Sofia fiddled with her necklace, a gift from her father after she had convinced a high-ranking gentleman that the bread her father sold him would take longer to mold, not that it would *never* mold. The lord had walked away with a partial refund and her father hadn't gone out of business. He had shown his gratitude by buying her the necklace. "It's yours," she said, lifting it over her head and placing it in her savior's outstretched hand. They took it and held it up to the fire light, a grin flitting across their face.

"Lovely, lovely. Now the fun begins."

Sofia lay down on the straw and watched the stranger take a seat at the spinning wheel. *Whirr whirr whirr*, it went; three times around and the reel was full of sparkling gold. *Whirr whirr whirr*, again, and the second reel filled too. Thus the hours passed with the hypnotic sound of the spinning wheel until Sofia fell asleep.

She woke the next morning to the sound of a key in the door. When she sat up, she found the room no longer filled with straw, but mounds of gold. The door opened to reveal the king, followed by the prince, princess, and several guards, all of whom stopped to take in the shining display.

"Well," the king said, his lips twitching into a smile, "it appears your father wasn't exaggerating."

"Does this mean I have to marry her?" the prince asked.

"Perhaps," the king mused, staring at Sofia. "But we need to make sure this wasn't a fluke. Guards?"

This time, Sofia was escorted by guards up to a tower, the king in the lead. "I knew you could do it if you put your mind to it," the king said as they climbed the stairs. "The offer to marry my son or daughter still stands; you could be queen. With your skills, our kingdom would prosper."

Sofia pressed her lips together. She knew agreeing to marry into the royal family would put her firmly at the king's whim. Even without the emotional blackmail, she was still not interested in the prince or princess. She never felt attraction the way the storybooks described it, but that didn't make her wrong or broken.

She was happy. She didn't need another person to complete her.

The king ignored her silence and opened the tower door. Sofia entered to find a large room, this one also filled with straw. It again had a spinning wheel in the center, but she was graced with a small bed and window this time, along with a fireplace. "We'll see what tomorrow brings," the king said in parting.

Sofia again sat down at the spinning wheel. She picked up a handful of straw as she had seen her protector do the day before and attempted to recreate what they did. The dry straw rushed through her fingers, and she thought she saw a flash of gold before the straw sliced her hands open.

"Ow!" She stopped spinning and pressed them into her apron, staining it with blood.

"That's not how you do it," came the same sing-song voice from the previous night. The stranger sat in the window, long legs dangling.

"You came back!"

"Don't sound so surprised." The stranger spun their legs into the room and joined Sofia at the spinning wheel. "I knew I'd be needed again. A king's greed is not easily tempered by a single room full of gold."

"Can you help me again?" Sofia asked.

"I can. If you have payment."

Sofia looked down at herself. "I have a ring," she offered.

The stranger glanced at the plain silver band. "Hardly worth anything really."

"It's worth more to me than the necklace you took last night," Sofia said, knowing somehow that the stranger valued emotional attachment more than monetary value. "It was my mother's ring, the only thing of hers I have."

A smile spread across her protector's face. "That will do, then," they said.

Sofia removed the ring and gave it to them. Before she knew it, the spinning wheel was once again going *whirr whirr whirr*, straw turning to gold before her very eyes.

"Could you teach me?" she heard herself ask.

Musical laughter was the only response.

Sofia sat on the bed this time, watching and listening as the spinning wheel went *whirr whirr whirr* and filled up reel after reel with shining gold. Sometime around midday, a guard brought her a simple meal, which she gladly shared with the stranger. She stayed awake watching them work as the fire turned to glowing coals and dawn touched the horizon. Only then did sleep overtake her. She again awoke to the sound of the door being unlocked. The stranger had once more disappeared while she slept, and Sofia scowled. She wanted to know more about them.

The king and his entourage entered the room, his face alight from the morning sun sparkling off the gold. "Well done."

"Does this mean I have to marry her?" asked the princess.

"Perhaps," the king responded again. "I have one more test, and then she can marry whomever she wishes."

Sofia balled her hands into her bloodied apron. "I still do not wish to marry either of you," she said to the prince and princess.

"Then perhaps you will marry me," replied the king.

As they had the previous day, the guards escorted her through the palace, this time going further and further down until they came to another closed door. This led to a giant room filled with straw and a spinning wheel. No fireplace or windows warmed the chill stone, but a comfortable bed adorned one of the corners. Sofia shivered in the cold and glanced at the king. "Spin all this into gold and your wishes shall be granted," he said, his tone icy.

"Will you let me return to my father?" she asked.

The king's silence answered her question and he shut the door behind him.

Sofia had barely sat at the spinning wheel before the stranger appeared. "I knew you'd come," she said.

The stranger quirked a smile. "And how did you know?"

"You like a challenge," Sofia said matter-of-factly. "But I have nothing to give you this time."

"The king wishes you to marry his son or daughter. He may even marry you himself. If you are to become queen, I would take your first born child as payment."

Sofia opened her mouth and heard herself say, "No."

The stranger looked shocked. They were not in the habit of being told no. "What?"

"I said no," Sofia said, crossing her arms over her chest. "I'm not marrying the prince, I'm not marrying the princess, and I am certainly not marrying the king, a man old enough to be my father. Even if I wanted to, I could not give you the price you ask."

The stranger studied Sofia as if they saw her for the first time. "You would give up your life for this? For you know that is the price the king will ask."

"I am not interested in the prince or princess," Sofia replied. "I'm still valid, and should be respected. I should not have to choose between who I am and my life."

Her protector was silent, studying her. "You are valid," they said at last. "Forcing you to marry is not going to change you. You are being given a choice to give up who you are or give up your life. I didn't see that."

"*Thank you.*"

The stranger gestured to the spinning wheel. "Sit," they commanded.

Sofia did as she was told.

"Take a handful of straw."

Sofia again obeyed.

"Begin to spin like you did yesterday, but give it an extra *twist* as you do."

"I don't—"

"Now."

Sofia picked up a handful of the straw and mimicked what she had seen the stranger do the previous day, giving it an extra *twist* as she did. Before her eyes, bits of straw turned to gold. She did not spin as well as her savior, but she could see the gold shine through.

The stranger smirked and bid her to stop. "You have a lot to learn, but you have talent. That shows your *willingness* to learn. Most of the people I help never get that far. They wait for me to do it for them, to save them from their fate. I make you an offer: If you guess my name, I will give you a gift such as I never have before. I will take you on as my apprentice."

Sofia gaped at her protector. "But I'm just the daughter of a baker. Surely your apprentice should be someone with more skill."

"You are more than just someone's daughter," the stranger replied. "You get to choose who you are, how to make yourself your own person. I will help. *If* you guess my name."

She could still do nothing but stare. "You're a little odd, aren't you."

The stranger's face lit up with a wicked grin. "Odd I am, yesterday, today, and all the days of my life. Very clever of you, to have plucked it out of the air with no help at all! With luck like that, you'll make a perfect student. Come, I have much to teach you."

"But I have not guessed your name."

"Oh, but you have."

Sophia paused. "Odd? Your name is Odd?"

"At your service," Odd bowed to Sofia and gently tapped on one of the stones in the wall with their heel. A doorway opened up and they gestured for her to go first. "Shall we begin your journey?" they asked.

Sofia grinned, and took the first step into her new life.

Expectations
by Bec McKenzie

In a way, this is many fairy tales, but may be best described as a vignette from "The Prince and the Pauper," a story by Mark Twain.

In the highest room of the tallest tower known to the many kingdoms, Prince Aldric of Devoira was having a crisis. This crisis had nothing to do with the innumerable dangers he had faced to reach this fabled tower, though they certainly didn't help matters.

Through the course of his journey from Castle Devoira to the oh-so-invitingly named Forbidden Tower, Aldric had been accosted by ruthless brigands, hideous trolls, and, on one memorable occasion, a fluffy but deceptively vicious little dog. All this, so that he might rescue the fair Princess Giselle. He didn't even particularly want to do it, but his parents had forced him. His father had gone on an adventure at his age, which of course was how he met his mother, so it was only natural that Aldric carry on the grand tradition.

"Ah, yes," Aldric scoffed. He stopped pacing to address the sleeping princess. "It always comes back to tradition, doesn't it?"

Princess Giselle, still sound asleep, did not reply. Feeling like a fool for ranting at no one, Aldric approached her bedside. Tradition also demanded that he break the curse upon her by placing a kiss upon her lips. As princely quests went, it was one of the easiest— provided, of course, one ignored the torment and humiliation he had endured to make it to her bedside.

This was supposed to be the easy part, the fun part. He personally knew half a dozen men who would either kill to be in his position or give him a congratulatory punch him in the arm. Princess Giselle was renowned for her beauty. Many lengthy verses of poetry had been written by those same men in praise of her fair skin and flaxen hair...but Aldric was terrible at poetry. In spite of all the efforts of his tutors, he lacked both the imagination and the vocabulary for it. He was never even certain what flaxen meant, but now that he gazed upon the princess, he had to assume it meant blonde.

Even if he didn't quite have the words to adequately describe her, Aldric had to admit Giselle was lovely to behold, so lovely that he really shouldn't have had such difficulty with this final step of the quest.

All it took was a kiss. Not even true love's kiss— such lofty romanticism had faded since in his grandfather's days—just a kiss.

"Right," Aldric said to himself. "Easy."

His stomach churned as he moved closer, perhaps because he had run out of rations two days previous. He remembered to remove the absurd adventurer's cap his father had given him only after his shadow fell across Giselle's slumbering form. The feather would just get in the way.

As he leaned closer, Giselle sighed in her sleep, her lips parting ever so slightly. Aldric recoiled, pulling the cap tight against his chest as if to protect himself. He knew if his father was here, he'd yell about how absurd he was being and forcibly push Aldric's face against Giselle's. His father, a man of action, was forever disappointed that his son had ended up the opposite.

Perhaps it was the crushing weight of the expectations placed upon him that made Aldric hesitate, but that still didn't explain why the very idea of kissing a beautiful woman repulsed him so. Not even picturing her as an equally beautiful man helped. His stomach churned, sweat beaded on his forehead, and he wanted nothing more but to turn and flee.

And yet…

He had come so far, suffered so much. He couldn't just leave her, could he?

Aldric turned away from the bed. More pacing was in order, now with the added distraction of turning his adventurer's cap over in his hands.

Never mind what his father wanted. Perhaps the true cause of his anxiety was the fear he would be a terrible husband and even worse king. Neither were things he had ever given much thought. Up until this quest was forced upon him, he had done his very best to avoid responsibility altogether.

So what exactly did he want? Other than to be anywhere else in the world. He was still mulling that over when an ear-splitting shriek rent the air. A figure rolled through the window with a cacophony of breaking glass and clattering armor. The source of the shriek was also the means of the knight's entry—a hideous, bird-like creature that hovered just outside the window.

Casting his battered hat aside, Aldric drew his equally battered sword upon the intruder and cried, "You won't take her!"

The words would have perhaps had more impact had fear and exhaustion not caused his voice to crack. Regardless, he was woefully outmatched, and no amount of bravado would help him. The intruding knight was clad in gleaming armor from head to toe, whereas Aldric's armor had been stolen by bridge trolls to use as dinnerware. That he had escaped from being dinner was a feat in and of itself, but it still left him with nothing but basic travel clothes.

The knight also had the flying beast on his side, whereas Aldric had been forced to eat his own horse.

And though he was proud of the family shortsword, so much that he took better care of it than he did himself, the knight had a massive broadsword…which he did not draw. Instead, he laughed. It was a distinctly feminine laugh that instantly made Aldric regret assuming he was facing another man, even if it *was* hard to tell under all that armor.

The knight removed her helmet, shaking loose her black curls with a flourish, and smirked at Aldric. He recognized that face.

"Shireen?!"

They had known each as children, brought together whenever one kingdom or another hosted a grand fete that demanded the presence of all neighboring royal families. When spying the two playing together, lords and ladies of the court joked they would make a nice couple—for if there was any justice in the world, Shireen's dark, aquiline features would cancel out Aldric's round, pale face to make for presentable children. It was a cruel jibe made by bored courtiers, but her parents took it to heart. From then on they were kept separate, lest any actual affection grow between them. In another world, such a ploy would backfire spectacularly, but such was not the case here.

It had been many years since Aldric had last seen Shireen. She had grown into a lovely woman, while he had grown from a round, pale little boy to a very tall, but still pale, man.

"Hello, Aldric," she said, as if they had only spoken yesterday. "You look like hell."

"Because I've *been* through hell!"

59

Realizing he was still brandishing his sword, and that his arm was growing tired, Aldric put it away. He cast a baleful look at Shireen's grotesque pet as it hopped inside to rest beside its mistress amidst the broken glass. "I didn't have some ugly flying monster at my disposal to just skip past the hard part!"

"Watch your mouth!" Shireen snapped. The bird squawked loudly. "Rudo's not a monster. He's my best friend and most faithful companion."

"Wait, *Rudo*?" Aldric frowned. "Why does that sound familiar?"

"Oh, I'm sure you heard mention of it here or there," Shireen said, turning away to pat her 'friend' on the head. His coat of glossy feathers terminated at his long, scaly neck, making it look like an overgrown vulture—except no vulture Aldric ever saw had a serrated beak. "I named him in loving memory of my betrothed, who died quite suddenly just before our wedding day."

She placed her hands on each side of the bird thing's head, though it didn't have ears that Aldric could see, and added in a stage whisper, "He was ugly, too."

The blitheness of her tone chilled Aldric. "Okay...but where did you even get that th—Rudo?"

"An engagement gift from the very same man," Shireen said. "No one is quite certain *what* dear Rudo is, but he *is* most certainly very loyal."

She stroked Rudo's beak.

"He was easy to train, and did a fine job terrorizing all the other suitors that came along." She leaned down and nuzzled Rudo's head. "After he nearly took one of their legs off, father let me do as I please."

"Great." Aldric swallowed hard. "I'm happy for you. So then why are you *here*?"

"So many questions." Shireen turned back to Aldric and folded her arms. "I'm here for the same reason you are, of course." There was a faint clink of metal on metal as she drummed her fingers on her elbow. "Which means I suppose we'll have to fight now."

"Wait, what?!"

"For the princess."

"But I was here f…no, wait, what am I even saying?" He made a sweeping gesture toward the bed. "Go for it."

Shireen arched an eyebrow at him. "Oh, so you fancy men, then? I always had a feeling, to be honest."

"That's not it at all!" Aldric snapped, bristling at the presumption. The anger shook something loose in him, a realization so sudden it left him feeling light headed. "I…I don't think I fancy much of anything, really."

Shireen stared at him, her dark eyes blank. After an uncomfortably long pause, she shrugged. "Whatever makes you happy, I suppose."

"What would make me happy," Aldric said, all the weariness of his travels creeping back, "is getting far away from here."

"And so you shall," Shireen said. "Just as soon as I—"

Giselle sat bolt upright in bed. "*SHUT UP!*"

Alric gasped. Shireen jumped back a step, and Rudo squawked loudly enough to make a stubborn piece of glass fall from the window frame. Giselle glared at them all, her face scrunched in abject disgust. Shireen pointed a finger at her. "You're supposed to be under a spell."

"And *you're* supposed to just get this over with!" Giselle turned her ire toward Alric. "First you come in here pacing and muttering to yourself for what felt like hours," she said, pausing long enough to round on Shireen. "Then *you* show up to…what?! Catch up?! Brag about the suitors you've maimed and killed?"

Shireen and Aldric exchanged looks. They spoke at the same time.

"There was no evidence I—" Shireen said.

"Well, to be fair—" Aldric said.

"No!" Giselle snapped. "There's nothing 'fair' about this! I've had to sit in this stupid tower pretending to be under a curse because my parents were too boring to piss off an enchantress and too cheap to hire one! Do you have any idea how long I've been here?"

Aldric looked to Shireen. She shrugged. Behind her, Rudo was preening himself, oblivious to the drama unfolding.

"Too long!" Giselle said. "I'm almost out of books, plus the food here is all preserved garbage! I might as well have been in prison this whole time! And then you two come along and make it even worse!"

"We're truly sorry about that," Shireen said. After a beat, she gave Aldric a look.

"Oh, right, yes! Sorry!" Aldric looked down at his hat, which lay in a sad crumpled heap on the floor. He didn't bother picking it up. "It's just, y'know, the way these things are done."

"Indeed," Shireen sighed. "All gallantry and daring-do and whatnot…I really expected it to be more exciting."

Aldric stared at his ruined hat—or rather, at his *father's* ruined hat. "So why do we even go along with it?"

"I don't," Shireen scoffed. "Not anymore. I just wanted to go on an adventure for a lark."

"That," Giselle said, "is an excellent idea."

She rose from the bed and smoothed her skirt. She was fully dressed and looked ready to attend a grand ball. Even her hair was perfect, but now Aldric knew she was prepared for their arrival—and had been for months.

Giselle looked downright tiny compared to the armor-clad princess, but nevertheless she squared her shoulders and looked Shireen dead in the eye. "I command you to take me home."

Shireen laughed. "Excuse me?"

Gizelle bristled. "Well, I'm not walking!"

Shireen, looking amused and intrigued, shifted her weight to one side. "This isn't how this is supposed to work, you know."

"Of course it isn't!"

Shireen folded her arms once more. "We're supposed to kiss first…traditionally."

Giselle raised a hand as if to smack her, thought better of it when her eyes fell upon Rudo. Instead she straightened her tiara. "Perhaps...*perhaps*...when we get to know one another better," she said, her anger giving way to a practiced loftiness. "But as it stands, I can't very well walk home. Thus I *humbly* request you escort me on that...whatever that thing is."

"Just call him Rudo," Shireen said, now thoroughly amused. She bowed with a flourish as Giselle walked ahead of her, and after a bit of struggling, Giselle relented and allowed Shireen to boost her up.

"Wait, so that's it?" Aldric said. "You're leaving together? Just like that?"

"She's *merely* my escort," Giselle snapped. She looked even more diminutive once Shireen settled in behind her on Rudo's back, and yet she was no less fiercesome. Aldric wondered if all the poets who likened her to delicate flowers had any idea of the real Giselle.

Shireen added, "We'll see how things go. It's a long way to the Castle Misnoia still."

"Put me in the middle of nowhere, will they," Giselle muttered. "I'll show them."

"Farewell, Aldric," Shireen said with a wink. The two of them really did deserve each other, Aldric thought.

Shireen clicked her tongue at Rudo, and in one smooth motion the great beast turned and leapt from the window. Giselle's yelp of fear quickly turned to a whoop of glee once they were airborne.

Aldric ran to the window after them. "Hey, what about me?!"

"You'll find your own way, I'm sure!" Shireen called back, her voice fading fast as Rudo reeled through the sky.

"Right...." Aldric's shoulders sagged. It was a long way back down the tower, and an even longer way back home, but that could wait until tomorrow. After carefully laying his sword aside, he threw himself on to the lavish canopy bed. Sleep took him gladly and swiftly.

)

The next morning Aldric awoke feeling more refreshed than he had in ages. It wasn't just that it had been the first night's sleep in a proper bed since his journey began. It was the absence of the weight hanging over him. For weeks he had dreaded what awaited him in this very tower, now that he was its sole inhabitant the only thing to fear was...what would happen when he returned home empty-handed. Somehow he doubted his parents would appreciate his newfound understanding of himself, particularly given he was the sole heir to the crown.

Taking a moment to mourn his very short-lived sense of relief, Aldric rose from the lush canopy bed, made a half-hearted attempt to smooth his rumpled travel clothes, and left the room behind. Unlike the journey upwards, when he focused solely on putting one foot in front of the other, he paid attention to his surroundings on the way back down the stairs. There were more rooms than the one at the tower's apex, as it turned out, and in them the deception of Giselle's kingdom became clear.

In the first room, nearest to the bedroom, he found a pantry with enough dried goods to stuff his empty satchel full. Next was a library filled with all manner of books, most of which were lying in stacks upon the floor. Finally, at the tower's base, there was a sparse recreation room. It contained an abandoned piece of inexpert needlework and a scattered deck of cards that could have been the result of any number of frustrations. Munching on a piece of jerky, Aldric left the tableau as it was and headed back out into the world.

It was a short walk back to the crossroads. Aldric's exhaustion and dread the day before had only made the last leg of the journey feel like it took forever. The marker at the top of the sign pointed the way he had come. It read *FORBIDDEN TOWER* in large gothic letters, while every other marker was plainly, sometimes even crudely, carved. Near the bottom of the signpost was the homeliest little marker of all, which also happened to point the way to the nearest settlement: Lump.

Aldric looked around. There was no one in sight in either direction—no one to encourage the idea that was forming, but neither was there anyone to discourage it.

"That's as good a sign as any," he said. No one was around to condemn the terrible pun, either, which only emboldened him further. Whistling to himself, Aldric turned away from the road to Devoira and instead traveled down the road to Lump.

The village was much smaller than anticipated, though he wasn't quite sure what he expected from a place called Lump. The village gate was little more than a rough arch stretching over the road. The sole watchman in sight, identified by his tarnished badge, was an old man who wasn't so much guarding the village as propping up the archway while he smoked his pipe.

"Ho there, Tad," he called. "Out for a stroll?"

Aldric stopped just short of the guard. "What?"

The ancient guard took the pipe from his mouth, as if that would help him see better, and leaned close enough to make Aldric recoil.

"Ah, beg pardon, sir," the guard said. "You're the spitting image of a weaver lad what lives down by the woods."

"I am?"

"Aye." The guard nodded and tapped his pipe on his knee. "If not for the posh clothes, I'd suspect y'were twins."

Aldric looked down at his battered travel clothes. He didn't think them very posh, especially considering how long he'd gone without washing them, but then he was very far from home indeed.

Another wild idea sank its teeth into Aldric. "And where does Tad live, exactly? I wanna see for myself."

The guard shrugged and pointed his pipe down the road. "Tell 'im Vern says hello."

The cottage of Tad the weaver lay a short walk beyond the village, at the edge of an idyllic forest that

67

looked like a scene out of a painting. The man himself was sitting on a stool just outside the door, also smoking a pipe. Aldric himself didn't smoke, had indeed never even considered smoking, but as he approached the cottage he thought perhaps he might take it up.

Tad indeed bore an uncanny resemblance to Aldric. The only noticeable difference was that while Aldric's black hair was a mess that defied all his best efforts, Tad's had the kind of perfect wave to it that actually looked befitting of a prince—and somehow, Aldric knew it was all with no effort on his part.

The idea that had been forming from the moment the old man misidentified him as Tad was ready to take flight by the time Aldric reached the cottage door and picked up the pipe that had fallen from Tad's mouth in shock. Once he recovered enough to invite Aldric inside, the two found it was easy enough to talk, though it quickly became apparent that looks were about the only thing they shared.

"Devoira?" Tad said, when asked of Aldric's village. "I've been there once, aye. For a tradeshow, it was. Brought my best wares for the journey. Had to fight off some trolls and brigands along the way, but that's nothing you don't prepare for, eh?"

"Right..." Aldric grumbled, rubbing a fading bruise from one of the trolls he had been grossly unprepared for. "Anyway, how would you like to go back? For good?"

Tad frowned. "I do a fair enough trade here. There's less competition, besides."

"No, not to be a weaver!" Aldric slammed his hands on the table, rattling the simple earthenware gloves. "I mean leave all of this behind, loom and everything! C'mon, haven't you ever dreamed of something more than all…" Aldric glanced around the tiny cottage. It was quite cozy, actually. "This?"

"Oh, indeed, sir…" There was a gleam in Tad's eye when Aldric looked back. "In fact, I've written a number of songs about it, if you'd like to—"

"No!" Aldric cried, with such intensity it startled Tad's cat awake. Up until that moment he had assumed it was a basket full of old wool. "I mean…No, thank you. I believe you. I can see it in your eyes."

"So what do you propose?"

"This," Aldric said, removing one of his gloves. Beneath it was the one thing of value he had left, after running into so many trolls and brigands. It was his royal signet ring, the undeniable proof of his birthright.

After several tries, and finally a bit of soap from Tad, Aldric removed the ring. The handoff was not quite as somber as he would have liked, but he suspected Tad still would have balked even if he got it on the first try.

"Oh, sir—I mean, your highness—I couldn't."

"I insist."

"But what if you change your mind? A weaver's life is dreadfully boring. Besides that, you don't even know how to weave!"

"So I'll learn." Aldric felt a pressure on his foot and looked down. Tad's cat, a massive cream and white thing, had moved from the basket to flop down upon him.

"That's Lump," Tad said.

"The cat's named after the town?"

"No, the town's named after the cat." Tad smiled. "He's also the Mayor. Though technically this is the eighth Lump."

Aldric stared at the purring mayoral mass on his boots. He reached down at picked Lump up. The cat stared back at him with supreme disinterest, but kept purring.

"That's it," Aldric said. "We're doing this. A village in the middle of nowhere—"

"Hey!"

Aldric cleared his throat. "I mean a quaint little township with a cat for a mayor is the furthest I can get from living in a palace. We have to do this."

Tad folded his arms. "And what if I change my mind?"

"Then I'll respect your decision, but I'm not going back. And besides, somehow I doubt you'll get tired of all the galas and the grand tournaments and the princesses."

"Princesses?" Tad's eyes lit up.

"Gobs of them. You'll have to fight them off with a stick." And for the better-looking version of him, that might even be true.

"But why?" Tad said. "Why give up all that?"

Aldric sighed and rested Lump in his lap. "Because I don't want any of that. I don't want princesses—or princes, before you say anything—or galas, or…any of what they expect of me, really. I just wanna be left alone, to do my own thing."

Tad was baffled. "And you'd really be happy like that?"

Aldric looked at the cat in his lap. Lump was already asleep. He smiled. "Look, I don't expect you to understand. I'm just starting to understand it myself, but yeah, this is the only way I'll be happy. Now take the damn ring, and when you get to Castle Devoira...I don't know, tell them you hit your head or something. They'll go along with it, I'm pretty sure. Hell, they'll probably be happy you're not me."

Aldric stroked Lump. He felt a bittersweet mix of emotion knowing they'd rather have a different version of him back home, but it was still better than what he felt when he was there, slowly being crushed under the weight of what they expected of him.

Tad, meanwhile, was brimming with excitement.

"I'll start packing now," he said, rising from the table. He was scarcely two steps away before he turned back. "And you're sure you don't want to hear the song?"

"Even more certain than I am of this."

And though there was no singing, they all lived happily ever after, nevertheless.

Li Chi and the Dragon
by Saffyre Falkenberg

This story is a retelling of the Chinese fairy tale
"Li Chi Slays the Serpent"

In the lazy heat of the afternoon sun, I sit against the rough trunk of a tree and nibble at the rice balls soaked with malted sugar that I packed as a treat. Beside me, Yanmei sighs and licks her sticky fingers, one at a time. She shifts, trying to get more comfortable in the shade of the branches, and I am keenly aware of her leg brushing against mine. When she has settled, she turns to me, beaming, and points out a brightly colored bird darting through the sky. I do not know whether it is the

73

balmy weather or the sweet rice balls, but something about the day is making me feel sleepy and content.

However, my mind soon wanders to more unpleasant places.

It is almost time for a girl to be sacrificed to the dragon again.

When the dragon made its home in the Yung Mountains, it demanded to be fed the flesh of a woman, a maiden. At first, people tried to kill the creature or give it their finest oxen and goats. It massacred the kingdom's finest warriors. In fear, the people gave in to its request.

Every year, a girl is sent by the officials to a temple built outside of the dragon's cave. They watch as the girl is devoured by the creature, to make sure that it is satisfied by their offering. This has been going on for nine years. Soon it will be ten.

I am the youngest of six girls in my family, and I am afraid. Not for myself, or my sisters, although, I suppose it is selfish of me to not be concerned for my siblings' safety.

The person I worry for the most is Yanmei. She lives on the neighboring farm with her parents and brothers, and she is the most beautiful girl I have ever seen. Every time she crosses my path, I try to memorize her features: her silky hair, bright eyes, wide smile, cheeks the color of peonies. The tinkling sound of her laugh brings me a joy like no other. I love her; the kind of love that most of the girls in my village feel for boys. Whether she feels the same way, I do not know.

I fear that her beauty will make the officials believe that she is a desirable sacrifice for the dragon.

That is why I have decided to volunteer myself. Her life will be safe for another year, at least. Right now, that is as much as I can give her.

I cannot tell my parents that Yanmei is the reason I am volunteering for this. They would not understand. So I tell them that I am sacrificing myself because they have no sons and, as the youngest, I am a burden on their house. It is an unfortunate fact that men are valued highly for their ability to work, while the efforts of women are ignored.

I do not believe in the truth of my words, but I must make them believe me, and agree.

)

We are eating dinner around the table in our farmhouse when I decide to tell them.

My mother drops her chopsticks on the floor in surprise, while my sisters exchange looks and say nothing.

"Chi, I will not let you do this," my father says. "Your mother and I love you."

"I love you, too," I whisper, staring down at my plate.

"None of you girls are a burden, do you understand?"

My sisters nod. I continue staring at my untouched rice.

My mother says, "We may not have had any sons, but we don't love you any less because of that."

"What else can I do for you, if not this?" I ask.

"Don't let such thoughts enter your mind. They are unwelcome guests in this home," my father says. With that, he stands up and leaves the house. I can see him walking towards the fields through the grubby window.

Even though they do not agree with me, I know the city officials will let me volunteer. Why choose an unwilling victim, when there is a girl waiting to take her place? The next day, I leave very early in the morning and tell my mother I am going to the market in the city. Thankfully, the city is not very far from my village, and I arrive before the heat of the day.

While I walk, I carefully consider my plan. Even though I will sacrifice myself to the dragon on Yanmei's behalf, I do not actually want to die. I am young, and should have plenty of life to live ahead of me.

Perhaps I could try to kill the dragon.

I think on this for a long while as I journey through the city. While I do not possess more brute force than the soldiers that have gone before me, maybe my cleverness will be my good fortune.

I find my way to the government buildings and tell the guard why I have come. He looks surprised, but he goes inside to inform the magistrates. When he returns, he takes me inside with him. I am too nervous to pay attention to the opulence of the building.

Two other guards standing outside beautifully ornate doors pull them open when I arrive. There is a group of six richly dressed men sitting around a table covered with paper and calligraphy ink. They look tired, as if they haven't slept in days.

The chief magistrate immediately asks me, "You wish to volunteer as the sacrifice to the dragon?"

Without hesitating, I say, "Yes, I do."

"That certainly makes our job much simpler," one of the other magistrates says.

"When the time comes, we will send a delegation to fetch you from your home and escort you to the mountain."

I nod. Then, in a fit of boldness, I say, "Your Honor, may I make a request?"

The chief magistrate pauses for a second, and then nods.

"On the day I am sacrificed to the dragon, may I have a hunting dog on a leash and a sharpened sword in a sheath? And may I have the freedom to use both of them?"

He narrows his eyes. "It is the least we can do, considering that you have volunteered for this terrible fate. But I feel I must warn you that these things will not be of any use to you. The dragon has killed some of our kingdom's finest warriors. A dog and a sword will not save your life, Li Chi."

I nod, but he does not know my plan. While I doubt it will work, I would rather die fighting than allow myself to be killed by this monster. Either way, Yanmei's life will be saved.

❯

On the first day of the eighth month, I am ready. My parents and sisters go about their chores as if it is a normal day. I feel heartsick that I haven't been able to tell them that this morning will likely be the last they ever see me, but I cannot bring myself to say the words. When my mother serves breakfast, I try to eat it, but my stomach is already full of fluttering butterflies.

I went to Yanmei's house yesterday. My intention was to tell her how I feel, because I wouldn't get another chance. But when I looked into her eyes…I just couldn't. Some horrid creature had grabbed my tongue and wouldn't give me back control.

We spent the day together, though. Just the two of us. Talking and laughing as always, and exploring the woods beyond the borders of her family's property. As the day grew old, we climbed a tree and watched the sunset together, shoulder to shoulder.

This is the memory I shall hold closest when I face the dragon.

Later that night, I had snuck back to her house with a letter that explained everything. My feelings, the dragon…all that I had wanted to say to her, but couldn't.

There is a knock on the door that startles me out of my thoughts.

"I'll get it," I say, wiping my sweating palms on my shirt.

Of course, it is the delegation sent to take me to the Yung Mountains. When they say why they are there, my mother bursts into tears. My father's face turns bright red, and he starts yelling. At me, at the delegation, at the dragon.

I clasp his hands and look into his teary eyes. "It is done," I say, trying to smile for him. I want him to be able to remember my smile when I am gone. While my father continues to shout at the delegation, I retrieve a small pack with a change of clothes and the other piece of my plan: a pack of rice balls soaked in malted sugar. As I start to walk out the door, my mother falls to her knees and grabs the hem of my clothes, sobbing for me to stay.

It breaks my heart to leave her like this.

I look across our fields and see Yanmei's house in the distance, and my heart warms.

Calmly, I leave with the delegation and begin my journey to the Yung Mountains. As promised, the chief magistrate gifts me with a sword and a dog. I attach the sword to my belt, and it feels heavy around my waist. Though I am not a soldier, I believe I will be able to wield this weapon when I face the dragon.

I am delighted by the dog. He is a large chow chow, all fluff and drool. Standing up, he would probably be the taller of the two of us. The chief magistrate says he has no name, so I decide to call him Gou, meaning dog. Not a very clever name, I'll admit, but the dog doesn't mind.

The trip to the mountain does not take as long as I expect. It is not even a full day's hike to the dragon's cave. I understand now why people are so afraid of this creature. If it wanted to attack, it could reach the village in the span of a heartbeat.

The temple they had constructed stands out like a sore on flesh. It is painted bright red, with gold filigree decorating the doors and walls. Thin pillars support the single-story pagoda. Though the temple is small, no expense had been spared. Gnawed bones and rusted pieces of armor litter the ground around the building.

There are metal shackles and chains on the front steps of the temple. There is still a foot and a leg bone in one of the cuffs. Looking at it makes me feel sick. Thankfully, because of my request to the magistrates, I will not be chained.

Gou whines at me, glancing between me and the mouth of the cave. He barks at the opening. I imagine he smells the dragon inside.

Death weighs heavy on the air here.

Now that we have arrived, the delegation retreats to a safe distance. None of them speak to me as they depart. I think they feel bad for me, or maybe they think I am stupid for volunteering for this fate. In any case, I cannot change my mind now.

I stare into the cave's opening, trying to see my enemy through the blackness. The dragon is nowhere to be found. Whispering a quick prayer to the gods for blessing and favor on my efforts, I clutch Gou's leash in my fist and approach the cave.

There is a great stink coming from within, and Gou keeps barking. I am afraid he will antagonize the creature before I can lay my trap. I kneel to the rocky ground and hurriedly unfasten my bag. Removing the parcel full of sugared rice balls, I begin to scatter them across the threshold of the cave. They smell sickly sweet, even to me, so I am hoping the scent attracts the dragon. Leading Gou away from the cave, we crouch behind a rock and wait for the dragon.

We don't have to wait long.

The dragon glides out of the cave, and my jaw drops. It is much larger than I imagined. Its scales are a glittery red, its body long and serpentine. Compared to the body, its legs are short and stubby, ending in sharp claws that flash in the sunlight. With eyes wide and glassy like mirrors, I expect that it is able to see me, even from my makeshift hiding spot.

However, it does not seem to notice me. It goes straight for the rice balls.

That's when I unclip Gou from his leash and send him at the beast. I say a quick prayer for his safety. Snarling, Gou charges straight for the dragon and leaps at it, all fangs. The dragon's head snaps up in surprise, right as Gou latches to its throat. Shrieking, the creature thrashes and I worry for a moment that the dog is going to be thrown off. Gou stays on, though, blood coloring the fur around his jaws.

Now it's my turn.

Fear paralyzes me for a brief moment. Am I really about to attack an enormous dragon?

I hold an image of Yanmei's joyful face in my mind. A faint smile on my lips, I sprint towards the creature, drawing my sword as I approach. I plunge the blade deep into the monster's neck. Deep burgundy blood spurts from the wound when I yank my sword out to deliver another blow. The dragon flails and screeches, front feet thrashing in the attempt to knock me and Gou away.

One claw catches me across the face, and I cry out in pain. Trying to ignore the hot blood on my cheek, I stab the beast yet again. The dragon jerks its neck hard, and Gou is thrown, slamming into the side of the cave's mouth with a sickening crunch. I cringe, believing the dog to be dead, but to my surprise and delight Gou darts up and throws himself at the dragon with renewed energy.

There is blood everywhere, covering my skin and clothes. It is hot and sticky, and I have difficulty seeing when it splashes in my eyes. I swing the sword, connecting with the dragon's face. It shrieks. I stab it in the head. The creature snaps at me, and I fall backwards to avoid its slavering fangs. I crawl away, trying to reach the boulder I had been hiding behind before. Weakly, I call to Gou to back off and come to me. I reach the rock, squeezing myself behind it. The dog joins me. His thick fur is matted with blood.

Breathing deeply, I try to summon whatever vestiges of energy still dwell within me. I doubt my fight with the dragon is over. Peering from behind the rock, I see that the dragon is struggling. It is wallowing in blood, drowning from the wounds in its throat. Now that I am away from immediate danger, I realize that I have stabbed the beast through the eye, but regardless, the fight is over.

It won't be long now.

I watch as the dragon dies, clutching Gou's warm body close to me.

Eventually, it stops moving, but I am too wary to approach it, for it is a clever monster. After what seems like hours, I finally gather the courage to examine the beast. It does not move as I grow closer. Standing next to it, I poke it with the tip of my sword to be absolutely certain that the dragon is dead. It does not react.

Waves of relief wash over me, and I can't help but laugh. Tears roll down my cheeks as the reality of my survival hits me. Somehow, with only rice balls, a dog, and sword, I managed to slay this serpent that has been terrorizing my people.

Before I head down the mountain to find my escorts and return to my village, I go into the dragon's cave to look for remains of the nine girls who had been sacrificed. The dragon has kept all their skulls as trophies. Solemnly, I gather them up and put them in my pack so they can be returned to their families and given a proper burial.

With Gou at my side, I begin the trek down the mountain, where the escorts are waiting to make sure the sacrifice goes as planned. When I turn a corner, the men burst out from a cluster of trees, pointing and shouting excitedly. Some of the guards run up to me and lift me up on their shoulders. Gou barks at them, tail wagging.

The chief magistrate stares at me with shock. "Is the dragon really dead?" he asks in a whisper.

"The dragon is dead. I collected the bones from the other girls, if you want proof," I say, handing him my bag. He peers inside, and shakes his head.

"Send a messenger down to the village. Spread the word that the dragon is dead, and Li Chi is alive. We are free!"

The men cheer, and one of the messengers jogs down the trail ahead of us.

Life is a whirlwind of events and emotions after I return home to my village. My family is overjoyed that I am safe, and my father won't let me out of his sight. Gifts pour in from across the nation, more wealth than I have seen in my entire life. The chief magistrate has even allowed me to keep Gou.

There are funeral services performed for the nine girls who were sacrificed to the dragon.

That is the hardest part. The families of all the girls approach me one by one after the ceremonies to thank me for giving them peace and allowing them to lay their daughters, sisters, nieces, cousins, and friends to rest.

I have not been able to bring myself to face Yanmei. After the things I wrote in that letter, I know things between us can never be the same. I thought I was going to die when I left it for her. Even though I have seen her many times in the village, I avoid her. I cannot bear to face her rejection.

I am at home when the offer comes. A missive from the king, to make me his wife, and the queen. I am sick from reading the words. My parents are exuberant. Their daughter, going from rags to riches.

Before they can notice, I quietly excuse myself and slip out the door. I do not know where I am going, only that I want to get away. Though he is the king of Yueh, I cannot imagine myself being married to a man. The very thought of it makes me feel too small for my skin.

In my dreams, my future is with another woman. My spirit longs for that woman to be Yanmei.

I find myself at the tree where we had watched the sunset the night together. Scaling the branches quickly, I sit on a limb where I can see the land stretched out for miles in front of me. Beautiful countryside and farmland, the small dots of my father's oxen grazing in the distance.

Yanmei's voice startles me. "I hoped I would find you here."

I have to grab the tree trunk to keep from falling. "Yanmei," I say, feeling ridiculous.

She grins at me, and my heart melts a little. "May I come up?"

"Of course." I scooch closer to the edge of the branch, so that she does not have to climb over me when she reaches our spot.

After a moment, she is sitting beside me, eye gleaming. "You've been avoiding me, Chi."

I feel my cheeks heat up. "Yes." I squirm.

"I was hoping you would come see me," she continues, "but I just couldn't wait any longer. I went to visit you, but your parents said you went for a walk. When they told me the news…about the king, I was hoping you would be here."

Tears fill my eyes, and I cannot bear to look at her. I am so ashamed of my cowardice. Somehow, I could defeat a dragon with a dog and rice balls, but I couldn't confess my feelings to the woman I love. My fingers drift to the scar on my cheek, a reminder of my fight with the beast.

"This is about the letter, isn't it?" Her voice is so soft.

I nod, unable to speak.

Then, to my surprise, she takes my hand. Her skin is warm and smooth, like that of a wealthy lady. I glance up at her, questioning her with my eyes. She only smiles. "Chi," she says. "I wish you would have told me sooner. All this while, I thought I was the only one."

I laugh; I can't help it. "That's what I thought. I didn't think there was anyone else like me."

Giggling, she shakes her head. Then she leans forward and kisses me on the lips. In that moment, I know in my heart that I am truly home. We stay like that for the rest of the day, sharing kisses and watching the sunset, sitting shoulder to shoulder.

As the sun sets over the horizon, I think about the king and his offer of marriage. Even though I don't know how my family will react, I know now for certain that I will refuse him now. If I could face a dragon in the name of the girl I love, then I could certainly face refusing the king.

Entwining my fingers in hers and sharing a smile in the new light of the moon, I know that my future is here with Yanmei, forever and always.

Satin Skirts and Wooden Shoes
by Moira C. O'Dell

A variation on "Cinderella," a story recorded by the Brothers Grimm but commonly said to be of French origin. Interestingly, the oldest known version of this tale comes from China.

The king and queen of a prosperous land were blessed with an infant son. The prince was comely of face, kind to his servants, generous to his father's subjects, and in all ways a dutiful and obedient son to his parents.

When at last the prince reached manhood, there came a time of much celebration throughout the realm, for the king and queen had chosen him a bride. The prince himself scarcely knew the maiden, having met her as one among many young ladies of good breeding with whom he had shared a dance at a courtly ball. Even so, bearing in mind his obligation to see the perpetuation of his lineage, the prince offered no objection to the match, and so the banns were published and the ceremony prepared.

However, the night before the wedding found the bride-to-be alone in her chambers, curled inward upon her stately bed and weeping bitterly. So mired was she in her distress that she neither saw nor heard the visitor who appeared in the room until the mattress dipped beside her and gentle arms drew her into a comforting embrace.

The maiden sobbed unquestioningly against the breast of her unknown comforter. When at last the storm of tears subsided, she raised her head to behold a wizened old woman whose eyes seemed at once old as time and young as a babe born yesterday.

Those eyes regarded the maiden with compassion as their owner said, "Dear heart, tell me: why do you weep?"

Fresh tears sprang to the maiden's eyes, but she choked them back and said, "Because I am to wed the prince upon the morrow."

"Is it not a joyous occasion, to be wed?" the old woman asked. "The prince is a man of good report who possesses the means and will to provide you with great luxury."

"Even so, I do not wish to marry him," the maiden said.

The maiden shrank back then in fear of the old woman's reply, but the old woman showed none of the scorn with which the maiden's guardian had met her objection. She looked thoughtful and said, "Could it be that your heart desires a princess instead?"

"It is not in my heart to desire such a match at all," said the maiden. "Not a prince, nor a princess, nor a spouse of any other station."

"Then heed well my words," said the old woman. "The liberty you desire lies not beyond your grasp, but you must strive for it with all your might, for others will seek to strip it from you.

"In the morning your maids will array you in your wedding finery and accompany you to the hall where the prince awaits. Before you leave this chamber, you must conceal beneath your gown the wooden clogs I shall leave you.

"When you reach the doors to the hall, a fanfare will signal the moment they expect you to enter. The sudden sound will draw the attention of your escort, and you must seize this moment of distraction to exchange your own shoes for the clogs. Your face, your skin, and even your gown will transform so that none will recognize you and you may make your escape.

"But this transfiguration will last only until the stroke of midnight, and the spell may not be renewed. The prince and your guardian will soon pursue you, so make haste to the ivy-covered mansion beyond the western walls of the city. Knock upon the door and tell your tale to the one who answers. If you trust her judgement, the mistress of the house will help you."

Without a word more, the old woman vanished. The maiden felt as though she might have dreamt the strange visit, but there upon the floor lay the promised clogs.

When morning came and the maiden's attendants arrived to assist her into her wedding gown, the maiden excused herself to the privy, that she might secrete the clogs beneath her petticoat. Thus prepared, the maiden proceeded to the doors of the great hall. She let her hope for escape shine upon her countenance as a look of eager joy, determined to give her escort no cause to stand too close or lay hands upon her.

The trumpets rang out, and doors to the great hall swung open. At the far end stood the prince, stately and handsome in his own wedding garb and with a smile of warm welcome upon his face.

Swiftly, the maiden bent and stripped away her shoes. She snapped the thread that held the clogs in place and slipped her feet into them. Her silken stockings sagged and darkened to coarse brown wool. Her flowing skirt withered to a threadbare apron covering the hard-worn dress that had once been her bejeweled bodice and lacy petticoat. The skin of her hands grew reddened and callused, and the reflection caught in a nearby windowpane showed her a face that might belong to any of hundreds of maidservants in the surrounding city.

The bridal attendants drew back in horror, and the maiden fled toward the palace gates. A clamor rose behind her, but she ignored it, darting first through the corridors, then through the throng outside who awaited the presentation of their prince's bride. Though she feared apprehension at any moment, at last the maiden escaped the palace grounds and emerged into the city.

Night had long since fallen by the time the maiden reached the western gate. She passed through unchallenged and at long last caught sight of the ivy covered walls of the distant mansion. Her feet ached in their unyielding shoes, but she forced herself onward without rest until she came to the door of the mansion.

Here, at last, the maiden's courage faltered. Perhaps those who dwelt within would return her to her groom, for surely the king would bestow a rich reward for the recovery of his son's betrothed. But the old woman's promises had thus far held true, so the maiden summoned her courage and knocked at the door.

A light bloomed behind the curtains in one of the second-story windows. A hand pushed the curtains aside, and the silhouette of a head and shoulders appeared, inclined as though to peer at the late-night visitor. Then the curtains swung back into place, and the maiden heard the faint sound of an inner door closing. A few moments later, a second, fainter light came into view through the glass panes in the outer door. The bolts slid back, and the door opened to reveal a tall woman of middle years, clad in a crisp white nightdress and bearing a single lighted candle.

"Whatever brings you here, child?" said the lady of the mansion.

"Please, do not think me mad," the maiden pleaded. "I have come here on the advice of one who can only be of the fair folk. Against my will, my guardian has betrothed me to the eldest son of the king. Today was to be our wedding, but by the intervention of the Fair One, I have escaped my captivity in enchanted disguise. The enchantment will fade soon, and the Fair One bade me seek your aid lest I fall into their hands once more."

The lady looked askance at the maiden's coarse clothing and toil-roughened hands. As fortune would have it, just as the maiden finished speaking, there came from the distant city the tolling of the great clock on the highest tower of the palace. Upon the twelfth stroke, the glamour fell away, revealing her delicate beauty and wedding finery. Only the crude clogs remained unchanged.

The next morning, the maiden and the lady sat together in the lady's private rooms. With much relief, the maiden had exchanged her costly garments for a nightdress of the same material as that of her hostess and found a restful sleep in a room set aside for guests.

"The Fair One did well to send you to me," said the lady. "I know what it is to wed contrary to the inclination of one's heart. My husband was a man of kindly disposition who provided well for me, and I much cherish my daughter, but had I the choice, I would not have chosen marriage."

Someone rapped politely at the chamber door. Without waiting for a reply, a young woman entered, bearing a breakfast tray.

"Good morning, mother," said the newcomer. "Oh, forgive me—I did not know we had a guest. If you will wait just a moment I…"

The daughter's voice trailed off into silence as she looked more closely at her mother's guest. The maiden could only return her gaze in speechless astonishment, for her hostess' daughter almost could pass for the maiden's own twin.

"My dear," said the lady to her daughter, "if you would, please prepare a meal for our guest. I will explain her presence while we break our fast together."

The lady's daughter listened in fascination to the tale of the maiden's plight. When the story ended, she sighed, "To marry the prince! I think I would welcome that match."

"Yet not everyone desires a match," the lady reminded her, "and those who do not should not be compelled to accept one. Could I have borne you and yet foregone marriage, I would gladly have it so."

The lady then addressed herself to the maiden. "I offer you indefinite shelter with a good will," she said. "I doubt not that those who would use you against your wishes will as likely seek you here as elsewhere. But fear not: the guise of a scullery maid has proven its worth once already, and clever costume will serve in place of magic."

Thus it came to pass that the maiden adopted the coarse garments, servile posture, and soot-besmirched face of a common kitchen maid. Her new mistresses treated her kindly and instructed the only other servant, the aging gardener, to excuse her elusive manner as the shyness of one formerly ill-treated by others above her station, and to leave her strictly alone. When the day's work was done, the three women—in careful privacy—took much pleasure in one another's company. Regardless of the maiden's nominal status in the household, the lady soon developed a great affection and kinship for her matched only by that for the lady's own daughter.

For the daughter's part, nothing gave her greater pleasure than hearing the maiden's tales of life in the wealthy heart of the city and the opulence of the royal palace whenever their household chores brought them together. She most loved all that the maiden could recall of the wedding preparations, and often went in secret to admire the wedding dress in its hiding place in the attic.

Perfect peace eluded them, however, for the day following the maiden's flight from the palace the king issued a proclamation declaring the prince's bride the victim of wicked magic and promising honor and wealth in exchange for her safe return. Those who witnessed the spell agreed that the magic had changed her garments and visage only, not the proportions of her body; and so the prince himself embarked upon a quest amongst all the dwellings in the land, seeking a maiden whose foot perfectly fit the shoes she had left behind, for the cobbler had crafted those shoes for her alone.

Inevitably, one day there came a herald commanding on behalf of the king that those who dwelt within the mansion should make ready for the arrival of the prince. The gardener greeted him and conducted him with all haste to the lady. The lady gave thanks for his tidings and dismissed both men from her presence; then she summoned her daughter and the maiden and spoke to them urgently.

The lady sent her daughter to draw a bucket of water, whilst the lady herself led the maiden into the cellar. There she revealed a priest hole in which she bade the maiden seat herself. When the daughter arrived with the water, the lady stirred into it a quantity of medicinal salts. This she placed before the maiden and bade her soak her feet in careful silence until the lady or her daughter came to fetch her. Then the lady closed the hidden door of the priest hole, and together with her daughter returned upstairs to prepare for their royal guest.

When the prince arrived, he began to greet the lady with every show of courtesy, but he faltered into wondering silence when he caught sight of her daughter. Hope bloomed upon his face, and the daughter flushed prettily and smiled in return. A footman stepped forward bearing a cushioned stool onto which he guided the daughter to sit. Then the prince himself took up one of the shoes left behind by his bride and, with utmost respect for the daughter's modesty, knelt and guided it onto her foot.

The prince's look of hope withered to disappointment, and the daughter's face followed suit, for her foot overhung the sole, bowing the supple fabric outward by a slight but unmistakable margin.

The prince gently reclaimed the shoe and rose to his feet. Addressing himself to the lady, he said, "My herald had word from your gardener that you employ a maidservant. Pray bring her to me that I may test the fit of the shoe upon her foot."

"Certainly, highness," said the lady. "I am yours to command; but I pray you, treat her gently, for she is a creature of slow wit and much mistreated by her former masters."

At her mother's bidding, the daughter descended into the cellar and opened the priest hole. The maiden begged the daughter not to compel her to face her unwanted bridegroom; but the daughter assured her that all would be well if only she held true to her disguise.

The daughter and the maiden returned to the presence of their royal guest. As the maiden paused, shivering, in the doorway, the daughter seized the moment of distraction to slip from the room and make her way upstairs. The prince eyed the soot-smeared, shrinking maiden with neither recognition nor expectation; but he offered her a kindly smile and spoke soft words of reassurance whilst he guided her to the stool and slid the shoe onto her bare and trembling foot.

The maiden covered her face with her hands, despairing that her disguise should be so easily undone; but the prince only sighed wearily. The maiden opened her eyes and cast her gaze downward. To her surprise, the shoe hung loose about her foot, for the chill water and astringent salts had shrunken the flesh.

The prince removed the shoe and rose once more. "My thanks, good mistress," he said to the lady, "for your hospitality and assistance. I now take my leave; for so long as she remains lost, I fear for the well-being of my bewitched bride, and I must not tarry in my quest lest delay bring her further harm."

"But I am lost no longer, my betrothed."

All eyes turned toward the door to the stairwell, where stood the daughter arrayed in the maiden's wedding garb, which fit as though crafted for her in truth. The prince's breath caught. He lifted a hand as though to reach out to her, and she in turn drew nearer.

"Can you doubt me still, my prince?" said the daughter. "Look upon my gown of satin, the circlet of silver upon my brow, the stockings of finest silk upon my feet. Am I not the bride you beheld when the great doors opened? Will you judge by the fit of a shoe that mayhap has grown distorted by the feet of many hundreds of women; or by the finery which only your bride has ever worn?"

Overjoyed, the prince caught the daughter in his embrace. "How came you here, and why remain hidden for so long?" he said. "Can it be you feared I would renounce you for the sake of your altered appearance?"

"The spell cast upon me left me confused and wandering," said the daughter. "Even now, there is much of my life beyond my power to recall. But the lady of this house gave me shelter while my mind and true form returned to me. And now the time has come for me to return to you, my betrothed."

Still clasping the daughter close, the prince gave profuse thanks to the lady for her kindness and pledged that the promised reward would come to her without delay. At the daughter's prompting, he assured the lady of her welcome at the wedding that would take place as soon as might be. Then the prince and his new bride-to-be departed, leaving the lady and the maiden alone.

The lady watched the royal carriage dwindle into the distance until at last it vanished behind the city walls. Then she turned from the window and settled into an armchair, head bowed and shoulders quivering. Tentatively, the maiden knelt at her feet and reached out to clasp her hands. The lady's breath hitched.

"He is a gentle and kindhearted man, is he not?" the lady said, wiping away tears.

"Of that I never felt doubt," said the maiden. "It brought great strife to my heart, that I could not desire him as I should."

"Never think that you *should* desire anything, child," said the lady. "Only you yourself can know what path will bring you happiness. My daughter will be happy, I believe, though it tears at my heart that I must henceforth play the part of a charitable stranger to ensure it will be so. And you also will know happiness, or so I hope. Will you remain with me? Not as a replacement for my daughter, but as an adopted heir, no less beloved. Or if you would not, the king's reward I freely give to you that you may begin your life anew wherever you wish."

The maiden paused. "The desire of my heart is to remain," she said. "But I cannot find it in myself to provide an heir of my body to follow after me. What would become of your estate when I pass on?"

The lady smiled through her tears. "Perhaps before that happens you will wish to adopt in turn."

Match Sticks
by Minerva Cerridwen

A variation (and, indeed, an evolution) of Hans Christian Andersen's "The Little Match Girl."

The little girl had been starving. On the threshold of death, she dreamt about striking the bundle of matchsticks in her hand, but her frozen fingers were too numb. She had already lost consciousness when she was found by an old woman, who carried her home and gave her blankets, bread, and hot milk.

In the morning, the woman asked how her young guest had come to be in such a dire position. The girl replied that initially it had been a relief when her mother sent her off to sell matches. It meant she would be away from her father, who was cruel to her. She was a disappointment, she explained, because he had wished for a son instead of a daughter. No longer wanting to make him so angry, she had wandered from village to village, further and further away, hoping that someone would buy a bundle of matches so she could afford a meal.

The woman's shock and rage at her parents' behavior reminded the girl distinctly of her late grandmother. She, too, had always claimed that all children deserved a proper home and someone to look after them. But when this woman, a stranger, offered to let her stay until she found a better place, the girl could not accept. She was too afraid that she might inconvenience her savior.

Eventually the woman agreed to let her pay for the use of her spare mattress. However, if the young boarder needed an income, she would have to sell something other than matchsticks. Something that people actually still wanted these days. And then the woman had an idea. There was one thing people wanted at all times: love.

A few potions, some quick spells, and she had rendered the girl's remaining matchsticks useless to light a fire. Still too weak to protest, the girl had been watching in a daze as she worked, but the woman assured her that the sticks had merely gained a new purpose.

They had become Match Sticks. As soon as a stick was put on someone's palm, it would move like a compass needle to point at the buyer's true love. If the girl went out selling these, she would never be ignored.

She only had to make sure she wore gloves at all times. The Match Sticks wouldn't work on the kind witch herself because she was the one who had enchanted them—but if the girl accidentally touched them, they would show the path to her own true love and become useless for sale.

The girl thanked her over and over again. When a few days later she had regained her strength, she ventured back onto the street, wrapped up in the gloves and warm clothes knitted by the witch. Yet it was her boots that she treasured most of all, even though they were far too large, because she remembered how painfully cold her feet had become on New Year's Eve.

At first, the girl's call of "Match Sticks! Match Sticks!" earned just as little attention as it had before. It seemed that the witch had been too optimistic.

Then the girl realized that they still looked like ordinary matchsticks and she changed her approach. "Find your true love! Find your true love!"

And suddenly everyone would stop and notice her.

She sold the first Match Stick to the butcher's daughter. It promptly made the young woman cross the square, but in all her excitement she didn't pay much attention to her surroundings and so she didn't see the baker's son before their shoulders crashed together.

Stammering, she explained the use of the Match Stick, and the man's face made the Match girl giggle harder than ever before.

The word spread fast through the village, and by the evening she had sold a whole bundle of matches. In the next couple of days, even visitors from the neighboring villages came to see if the rumors were true.

And indeed: the tinker's true love turned out to be the seamstress; the toy maker fell in the cook's arms; a librarian from another village gathered courage to talk to the judge.

Yet the Match girl soon found that she was far more interested in the sticks' less predictable behavior. Perhaps it was because she was certain that her horrible father would not have approved of those stories. Or maybe it was the happiness of the two young women she met on the second day, when they realized that the sticks' magic acknowledged their love.

In the weeks that followed, the girl learned about the many forms love could take. The Match Sticks made it clear that true love would not be defined by traditions or rules. One time, a middle-aged woman's match even split in two to lead her to both her loves. And only a few days later, a farmer was tricked into taking a Match Stick by his wife. When it pointed at his best friend, she exclaimed: "See? I told you so! Now go kiss him and bring him over for dinner!"

The Match girl was a little worried by this turn of events, but a week later the wife came back to her, beaming as she explained that the three of them now lived together and that she had never seen her husband happier.

Every night, the girl returned to the witch's house with money to share and new stories to tell. The old woman would listen in surprise while she enchanted fresh bundles of ordinary matches. Even she would never have imagined that there were so many different types of relationships.

The two of them would talk into the night, and while the witch taught her about magic, the girl gradually learned how lonely her friend had been before her arrival, and how she appreciated her company. For the first time since her grandmother's death, the girl felt welcome and cherished. For the first time in her life, she had a real home.

That was why it shook her to the core when, after five months, she met her first angry customer.

What if the Match Sticks' magic was wearing off? What if she could no longer pay the witch? What if she had to leave?

Of course there had been some disappointments before. Everyone was always talking about the times when the matches showed someone's true love immediately, but many people had to walk for days before they met theirs. This led to a lot of frustration, which was fortunately forgotten as soon as they arrived where they needed to be.

And while the Match Sticks meant the start of many happy relationships, there were a few cases in which the customer's true love went unrequited. But even then, getting to know the person the stick had sent them to usually resulted in a great new friendship.

The sticks had also proven to be rather unpredictable. They wouldn't always lead people where they expected. One man had been so certain that he would be directed to his boyfriend that he had planned to use the match to ask his hand in marriage—only to find that instead, his true love was the pencil that helped him make the world a more beautiful place with his drawings.

To many others, it came as a relief that their true love was not another person. Quite a few people who had never been in love only came to the Match girl out of curiosity, or because a well-meaning relative had sent them. Would there be someone they were attracted to after all?

Almost always, it turned out that they knew themselves better than they were led to believe. The sticks brought them to their passions—the girl could immediately think of someone who'd been led to her piano, their kitchen, his cats—or to their best friends, whom they loved dearly, though not in a romantic way.

But the bulky man she met that day was so angry that he even started shaking her by the shoulders.

"You are a fraud!" he shouted, as the girl trembled in fear. "Months ago I bought one of your sticks and it sent me all around the world. I never met my true love! They do not work at all!"

She dropped everything and ran home, afraid of the man's rage. The witch was worried when she saw her return so early. When she heard what had happened, her mood turned to anger.

"That man was an idiot," she stated, "and I'll prove it to you!"

She dried the girl's tears and cheered her up with tea and biscuits, and then they went out together, hand in hand, to find the bulky man at the pub. A group of people had gathered around him as he recounted his adventures around the world, receiving lots of *ooh*s and *ahh*s at the many marvels he described.

"Not so bad then, those Match Sticks of mine," the witch said loudly when he paused for breath. "It sounds like they made you discover quite an extraordinary love: a passion for adventures and travel!"

Then the man realized that he would never have left his business behind if it hadn't been for the matches, and he apologized to the girl with a bag of coins so large that she wouldn't have to sell Match Sticks for several months.

But the girl still went out with her apron full of bundles every day. She loved the new discoveries customers made about themselves, and the fond smiles when the sticks confirmed that someone's partner of many years was indeed their true love. Besides, everyone in the village now knew her and stopped to chat, because often her matches had played an important part in the direction their lives had taken. Never again would she be hungry, for every single one of them would gladly invite her to dinner.

As the years went by, she sometimes wondered what would happen if *she* touched one of the Match Sticks. While she appreciated the beauty of many of the girls in the village, she could not imagine herself kissing them or holding their hands in the moonlight. She had many friends with whom she enjoyed long walks in the fields and winter evenings at the inn, and with whom she danced at the midsummer party on the square, but she was equally fond of them all. The thought of living with just one of them for the rest of her days terrified her. Their friendship would inevitably change, and that was the last thing she wanted.

She suspected that if she did use a Match Stick, it might spin endlessly in an attempt to point at itself, showing how much she enjoyed her daily occupation.

When she finally found out, it was an accident. All those years, she had been careful to wear the gloves, but lately her hands and feet had grown so much that even her old boots had actually become too small. On a sunny day, she was about to give a customer their match when her right glove slipped and the wood touched her bare skin.

Immediately the small stick turned over, landing on her palm, and the customer gasped.

"M-me?" they asked, looking slightly alarmed as it clearly pointed in their direction, but the girl had seen the Match Sticks at work for so long that she could tell this was not her final destination.

She apologized to the customer and carefully handed them a new match with her left, gloved hand. For once, she didn't stay to see what happened. She was too curious where she would find her own true love.

The match kept pointing forward as she walked over the square and through the streets of the village, until she reached the edge of the forest, where only one little house stood.

She opened the door and waited for the witch to look up from the herbs she'd been chopping. Then she held up her hand to show the match.

The old woman smiled. "I love you too, dear. You're home early today. Why don't you sit down so I can get you a cup of tea? And then I can continue to teach you about fire spells."

The girl felt warm inside as she sat at the kitchen table. Once again, the magic had got it right. While she loved to see how the Match Sticks brought couples together, she had no interest in becoming part of one herself. All she needed was here, at home, close to the friends and the village she cherished. This wise old woman had taken such good care of her, and taught her so much, that she probably *did* love her more than anything else. The girl could not have found a better match.

The Princess of the Kingdom of the Dark Wood
by Dominique Cypres

Based on the Brothers Grimm fairy tale "The Shoes That Were Danced to Pieces," this story has gone by many names. Most will find it familiar.

It happened that a young tailor who lived on the coast fell upon hard times. Accepting what little charity his friends and family could provide, he set out into the great forest upon a horse to find a new master who would accept him into service. After some weeks of traveling without so much as a helpful word, he came to a village where the innkeeper told him of a very small kingdom, further inland still and one week's travel away, where the king was in need of a tailor.

"The king has one heir," the innkeeper said, "a son who will complete his sixteenth year this autumn. The son is to take his father's crown then, and the preparations require an experienced tailor willing to work with thistledown."

The tailor doubted that his work could be deemed worthy, but he was in no position to turn down the opportunity. He set out upon the path described by the innkeeper. His journey continued on for five uneventful days. Soon after setting out upon the sixth, the tailor observed a thickening of the forest canopy. The trunks of the trees, too, drew closer together; the way became narrower and crowded with roots. Oak leaves choked out the daylight until nightfall passed almost unnoticed, so that the tailor had to make camp largely by rummaging about without the aid of his eyes. He ate his provisions beside a fire, but even the firelight seemed to penetrate the depths of the wood with less ease than the night before, dissipating feebly a mere yard or two from its source.

The tailor awoke at dawn. The sun was still a dim glow through the canopy, but he heard the chattering of birds. As he traveled on, the trees grew taller and denser still, until the tailor feared that he may not see his way without the aid of a torch; but just this fear entered his mind, he saw a lantern holding a slow-burning candle, hanging from a steady bough. As he passed it, he saw another, and then yet another, and so these lanterns continued for perhaps an hour of steady riding, until at last he spied a lantern swaying low to the ground. This last lantern was borne by an old woman out hunting truffles with her hog, and when the tailor had explained his business, she kindly led him to a clearing of sorts—still covered by that impenetrable canopy, but cleared of roots and undergrowth. Within this clearing lay the entire kingdom of the dark wood, aglow with lanterns, the castle at its center.

The tailor was welcomed into the castle, and at once met with the king. The tailor presented samples of his work with many apologies for their simplicity, but the king was well pleased.

"It is most magnanimous of you to travel so far to serve the court," the king said. "We have no true tailor to speak of, and my son has made the most unusual request to appear at his coronation dressed in local thistledown. But there is another matter. My son's cloak is forever in tatters. Every evening the queen herself mends it, and every morning, though my son has spent the whole of the night in his chambers, his cloak is torn nearly to shreds, and he acts fatigued, as though he hasn't slept a wink. I fear he has been unjustly cursed. If you can ascertain what has so worn the Prince and his cloak every night, you will be handsomely rewarded."

The tailor was then led to the chamber of the king's heir. The heir greeted the tailor warmly and bade the king and attendants leave them alone to soak by the fire by the fire. The youth then drew from the mantle a flute, and, handing it to the tailor, asked "What is this flute made of?"

"It is made of bone," said the tailor.

"Are you certain?" asked the heir.

"Yes, for I have seen such flutes at home."

"What if I told you it was made not of bone, but carved from ash?"

"I would believe it."

"But you were so certain before!"

"Yes, but the light of the fire is dim, my hands are numbed by many days of travel, and, after all, it is your flute."

The heir smiled, and said, "It is very well. Tonight I will show you where you must gather thistle for my coronation clothes. You must excuse me, but it will be easier to see in the dark of night." Then the youth retrieved the flute from the tailor's hands and began to play strange, lively tunes.

The tailor listened politely and with interest, but was weary from traveling, and soon fell asleep.

That night, he awoke, still seated by the fire, to the touch of a hand on his shoulder. The heir stood over him in a heavily patched cloak, and, seeing that the tailor was awake, bade him follow. The heir carefully knocked twice on a panel of the frame of the bed and all at once it sank below the floor, revealing a staircase leading underground. The heir took a candle and bade the tailor follow down these ponderous stairs. They walked down and down, so that they had long lost sight of the bed-chamber, and the tailor was sure that they must be deep underground. Just as they caught sight of an earthen passageway at the end of the stairs, a draft of air extinguished their candle.

The tailor cried out, and was ready to climb back all those stairs in the darkness, but the heir shushed him, and said, "We've no need of the candle now; look about!"

114

The tailor did as he was told, and soon his eyes adjusted to another source of light, a steady blue glow that seemed to emanate from all around. The passageway at the end of the stairs opened onto the edge of a vast subterranean wood, much like the one the tailor had traversed above. Its undergrowth was dotted with thistles like he had never seen, each glowing as if inhabited by an unwavering blue flame. More stunning, however, was the figure of the heir, who stood before the tailor and dropped the hood of the cloak to smile upon him.

For, by the curious light of the thistles, the tailor could see everything more plainly than he ever had in the kingdom of the dark wood above, and looking upon the king's heir in that light, the tailor knew her to be a beautiful young maiden, though she bore all the same features the tailor had seen when she had received him in her chambers above. The same eyes that had struck the tailor as handsome and princely above he now saw for what they were—the dark and beautiful eyes of a princess.

Struck by the heir's radiance, the tailor knelt at her feet. "Your Highness!" he exclaimed. "Princess of the Dark Wood! Surely I have done nothing to deserve this honor."

"Worry not," the Princess replied. "You will make a fine guest at the ball tonight."

The tailor dared not question her, and so without a word he followed the Princess onto a narrow road that led into the heart of the wood. The thistles grew ever thicker as they passed, and their light ever brighter.

Thorns and branches tugged at their clothes, tearing the princess's cloak again and again. Soon they came to a wide but placid river, upon which a boat was tethered and waiting. Not much sooner had they crossed this than a meadow came into view ahead, almost painfully awash in the thistle-light, with a great castle in its center.

"We are about to enter the underground castle of the Forest Folk," the Princess said, "unseen by any man and woman of the kingdom above, save myself." She produced her flute from a pocket and handed it to the tailor, who could see now without doubt that it was made of ash. "When you attend your first dance," she explained, "it is customary to present a gift to the Forest King."

Within the castle, a great party had already begun, hosted by the Forest People, who were neither men nor women. At its center, directing everything and attending to every guest was the handsome Forest King, who graciously accepted the flute from the tailor, and greeted the Princess as an old friend. The Princess and the tailor partook in a great feast of strange custard-like fruits and rich honey, and the Princess danced seven waltzes with the Forest King. The tailor caught his reflection in the strong cider he was given, and saw that, in the thistle-light, he looked a little more like a Forest Person than a man. The thought pleased him. The party dispersed, and the Princess and the tailor returned to the Princess's chamber, stopping at the river to gather as many thistles as they could into two great sacks the Princess had brought along.

In the morning, having slept but very little, the tailor and the Princess set to work spinning thread from the thistle. By day they spun and wove, and by night they feasted with the Forest King, until they had all the tailor needed to fashion the Coronation clothes. The Princess demanded that the Tailor be granted a room where he could work in private, and so he made an extravagant Coronation dress.

When time for the Coronation came, the Princess asked to be crowned at nightfall, and that she should enter the ceremony with all the curtains drawn and all lights extinguished.

The King began to grow impatient with waiting in the dark, and called out, "Let the Prince enter, so that we can all see again!"

Just then the Princess stepped into the room, aglow in her new thistledown dress, to the great astonishment of all but the tailor.

The King cried, "What have you done with my son?"

The tailor replied, "You need not worry for your son. Look! Now, for the first time, you can see your daughter."

"He speaks the truth," the Princess said. She had the curtains raised, and the candles lit again, and a flame lit in the fireplace, so that the glow of the thistledown could no longer be seen, but all now saw her as she truly was, and the King proceeded to crown her Princess Regnant of the Kingdom of the Dark Wood.

In return for his services, the tailor was offered the Princess's hand in marriage, but he declined, knowing that she had other wishes. He told the King he required no bride, and would ask only for a workshop in the kingdom. He was given this and a lifetime of unlimited hospitality, though he preferred a simple life and accepted only the humblest of accommodations. He wedded himself to his craft, and soon had clothed the whole kingdom in splendid thistledown garb like that worn by the beloved Princess. He trained apprentices, too, and for a time, thistledown cloaks and dresses from the Kingdom of the Dark Wood were worn by all sorts of people far and wide.

The Princess brought the King and Queen to feast with the Forest King in his underground castle, and then the other members of the court, and soon thereafter anyone who wished to visit. She led her kingdom into an era of great happiness, and married Forest King, and their peoples became one. They became more and more at home in the darkness of that forest, and had less and less need of anything they couldn't grow or craft themselves.

The road that leads to the Dark Wood has long since been overgrown, and no one now remembers the way, but it is said that lanterns of the Kingdom remain lit to guide anyone who comes seeking beautiful garments of thistledown.

Damma and the Wolf
by Kassi Khaos

This retelling is based on the European fairy tale commonly known today as "Little Red Riding Hood."

There was a small town in a valley between two mountains. Rather isolated, the town used the lake and thick forest nearby for their needs. The people who lived there were intensely protective of their young, vigilant that they didn't stray too far because of the dangers that surrounded them in the wild. All of the children had grown up hearing tales that left them with visions of what sharp-toothed horrors awaited them amidst the dark depths of the water and trees.

The land was enchanted in a way that would affect the people who lived there forever. In the deepest woods, words now carried magic, and all creatures now carried words.

To accommodate safe travel in the forest, the townspeople created a path that led to the most frequently visited areas. They lined it with torches to make sure travelers always had light if they needed it, as it got quite dark in the deeper parts of the forest. The children were usually safe roaming in daylight, but at night it was avoided by even the bravest of townspeople.

Except one.

They all called her Grandmother. She was the oldest person in the town, but she lived in the forest a little off the main path. She was adored and respected, often consulted by people young and old. She was the only one daring enough to live so far from town, though it was whispered that she was descended from a creature that used to stalk in the forest. Therefore, people were cautious not to upset her. Words could do much out there, especially words made in anger.

Many of the shops would deliver goods to her so that she didn't have to go to town. Young Damma was a shop girl for the baker. Her duties included going to Grandmother's house to deliver baked goods. Damma was affectionately called Red Hood by the townspeople, as she always wore a red cloak. It had been a gift from Grandmother when Damma had turned 14. The cloak was beautiful and well-made. It felt like being wrapped in a warm embrace every time Damma put it on.

Damma started on the familiar trek to bring Grandmother's deliveries, her red cloak fluttering gently behind her. The forest seemed almost unnaturally lit, but

Damma could still see the path enough to continue her journey.

Surprisingly, Damma was hardly ever uneasy in the forest. She had taken this trek many times and had come to have appreciation for the woodland. Today, though, it felt as if the trees surrounding her were watching. Damma looked carefully around and saw nothing, so she continued on her way.

Damma stopped briefly to pick a pretty monkshood flower. She handled it carefully, gently slipping it into her basket. She would give the token to Lily, who loved flowers so. With a distant smile, Damma continued on, her thoughts focused on her beautiful Lily.

Off in her own head, she hadn't noticed how dark and dense the forest had gotten. She floated on, reaching into the basket to stroke the petals. She had never gotten the same joy Lily had from handling flowers, but touching this one reminded Damma of Lily's joy, which made Damma happy.

Suddenly, Damma was tugged down and hit the ground with a bone-jostling impact. Looking up from where she lay, she saw a flash in the bush. She felt her throat constrict as fear started to wiggle its way into her mind. There were many things to be afraid of in this forest. Muddy and scraped, she got up on her knees, ignoring what she saw for now and looking behind her. Her cloak had gotten caught in some thistle by the path. It was torn. Damma felt her spirits fall. Even after she fixed it, the cloak just wouldn't be the same.

Looking around her warily, still sensing the foreboding atmosphere, Damma reached behind her to untangle the cloak from the thistle. She had almost gotten it free, which was doubly difficult as she had to untangle it with shaking hands, when she heard a low noise coming from the bushes in front of her. Her head whipped up to see another flash of dark brown and grey in the bushes. Frozen, she tried to listen intently for something, anything, but it was silent. More silence. Damma unfroze and moved to crouch. There was a rustle behind her but she didn't turn, afraid of what she'd find. She started to slowly rise when a wolf darted onto the path in front of her. Falling back in fear, Damma blinked up at the light brown eyes.

For a second, Damma saw Lily in those light brown eyes, but then it faded and she saw something else. No, Lily was not in those eyes. They held something much darker than Lily's would ever be capable of. Damma found herself wishing that they were Lily's eyes, but they weren't, and she wasn't going to be able to wish the wolf away. It started pacing in front of her, the intense brown eyes never leaving hers. Damma felt a chill run down her spine and the hair on the back of her neck rise.

"What are you called, little one?" The wolf had a deceptively kind voice. She knew that it would not hesitate to attack. Wolves were not known for their kindness. Damma knew the old tales, she knew not to trust a wolf.

A thousand warnings sprang into Damma's mind: whatever is spoken in the forest cannot be unsaid, lying can be just as dangerous as the truth, names hold power, and the most dangerous of predators used words that were coated with honey. "I am called Red Hood."

"A fitting title, certainly, but surely that is not your name." The wolf had started coming closer and Damma had little idea of what to do, but she knew not to give it her name.

"No, but I am called such." Her mind raced to find a suitable name. She then remembered what her mother had called her as a child. "Rosebud."

The wolf growled suddenly and sprang forth. It grabbed the basket which had been lying beside her. Damma winced when the wolf started pawing at it. The flower would be ruined, as would the rest of the contents. She had become quite attached to that basket. She was about to protest when the wolf spoke again.

"What is your name, child?" it growled, all the honey gone from its voice.

"Dearheart." Damma said instantly, her mind jumping on to what Lily often called her. "Leave, wolf. I have no name for you."

The wolf paused its growling, as if dazed or bewitched. Its head cocked, studying her a moment with the intelligent eyes. It then gave her a toothy grin and ran off through the forest.

Shaken, Damma gathered her basket—the flower was bruised, she noticed—and quickly hurried the rest of the way to Grandmother's house. She wanted to turn back, but that would have been even longer a journey. She wanted to go back to the comfort and familiarity of the town—of Lily. She hurried on, but trees seemed to jump out and cling to her, impeding her speed. When finally the house was in sight, Damma let out a breath of relief. She was hoping she could stay with Grandmother for the night. The journey back wasn't one she wished to start so late in the day. It was best to be inside at nightfall.

She knocked on the door and waited. She heard the rustling of someone inside, and then Grandmother opened the door with a smile.

"My dear Red Hood! You have my purchases? You are such a sweet girl for getting them for me!"

"Hello, Grandmother," Damma said with a pained smile, and followed the older woman in the cottage. "I'm afraid some of the rolls got smashed."

"Oh dearheart. You do look travel-worn."

"There was a wolf!" Damma said, shuddering at the memory. Grandmother clucked her tongue, and put a hand on Damma's shoulder leading her towards the kitchen, taking the basket.

"You poor dear, I think you need some tea."

Damma sat down at the table and began to tell her tale. Grandmother listened quietly as she prepared tea for them both, setting a cup in front of her visitor when it was done. Damma accepted the warm drink gratefully, taking a sip that felt beautiful on her throat, before continuing her story. She clasped the cup to her chest, hoping it to be a fragrant talisman to ward off her fear.

"You've had a quite a day, haven't you. You said your cloak was ripped. May I see it?" Grandmother asked, taking a drink of her own tea. Damma stood to take off the cloak, but she did so hesitantly. Taking off the cloak make her feel vulnerable—naked.

Grandmother took it with a shake of her head. "I should be able to fix that right up. Why don't you stay here and drink your tea while I go my sewing supplies?"

Damma stayed in the kitchen as Grandmother went further into the cottage. She sipped her tea and tried not to feel uneasy, reminding herself that she was safe with Grandmother. When she finished, Damma noticed how cold it had become and how silent the cottage was. Instantly, she was reminded of earlier and tensed. Something was wrong. Damma walked cautiously out of the kitchen and into the main area of the cottage. No one was there. Still, it was silent. Did she dare call out? Damma silently crept towards the bedroom, her eyes scanning the cottage in the dim light for any movement. She would not be hunted again.

Drawing closer to the door, Damma felt the hair on the back of her neck rising. She placed a hand on the slightly open door and pushed it open. It creaked softly. She saw a figure by the chest of drawers and felt like she would faint away, until she recognized the clothes. It was Grandmother. Damma gave a sigh of relief. Grandmother turned around swiftly, as if she had somehow heard the soft sound.

"Rosebud? Is something wrong?" Grandmother asked, drawing nearer to her.

"No, forgive me, I just wanted to see if you needed any help?" Damma smiled, feeling slightly silly for assuming the worst. Usually, Lily was there to reign her in, though Damma couldn't say she wanted Lily there with her. As much as Damma missed her, Lily was much safer in town.

"Why thank you, dear, how sweet of you. Why don't sit on the bed while I look for these darn sewing needles of mine?"

Damma nodded and sat down on the bed while Grandmother continued rustling around in the drawers. Damma still wished for the comfort of her cloak, but the bed was at least more comfortable than the wicker chair. Suddenly, Grandmother straightened and looked at Damma.

"My goodness, you smell like monkshood." Damma blinked at Grandmother. She had been in the patch of monkshood to pick one for Lily, but that was many hours ago now.

"What a keen sense of smell you have, Grandmother! Yes, I picked one for Lily, though..." Damma trailed off as Grandmother approached her. Something about the way she walked seemed familiar.

"Ah, yes. Sweet Lily, how is she?" Grandmother stood in front of Damma, looking down at her. Something in her eyes reminded Damma of Lily, but she couldn't put her finger on the familiarity.

"She's well," Damma said with a slight blush, wishing for the comfort of her cloak even more. She was starting to shiver. It was getting cold as nightfall approached. Grandmother trailed a hand up her arm, noticing the movement.

"Are you cold, my little Red?" Grandmother asked. Damma's eyes widened and she looked at Grandmother again. Those eyes didn't remind her of

Lily at all. They reminded her of something much more sinister—the wolf. Now that Damma had noticed the similarity, had Grandmother called her Rosebud? And dearheart? How had she known about those names? Damma felt the panic begin to rise.

"What interesting eyes you have, Grandmother," Damma said, the feeling of dread filling her again. Grandmother smiled a feral smile. Their eye contact broke as she looked down at Damma's frame, which shivered again in fear.

"All the better to see how lovely you are, my dear."

Damma didn't know what to do. She was thinking desperately about how she could get away. There had to be something she could do! Damma looked on with horror as the smile loomed closer. Had Grandmother always had such sharp teeth? Damma had not realized she had spoken until the last word left her mouth.

"All the better to eat you with, dear! Such a nice girl too, what a pity. You should have known to respect those of the forest." This was all the warning Damma got before Grandmother charged, tearing clothes and grabbing skin.

"No!" Damma cried loudly, sounding much braver than she felt. She closed her eyes in fright, desperately wishing to be anywhere else. The hands stopped suddenly and a silence descended. No hands pawing at her, as they had her basket not long ago. No growling. Nothing. Damma peeked open her eyes to see again the blur of a wolf streak past.

Damma stared in disbelief. It was over! Tears of relief started welling in her eyes. She was finally safe. Damma stayed on the bed until she saw light peeking through the window of the cottage. At dawn, she left the cottage without looking behind, cloak and basket in hand.

Over the years that followed, the story of the wolf was told many times to all the town's children, including those of Lily and Damma. For in the forest, names are best not spoken to hunters, and words have weight— especially the word no.

Beauty's Beasts
by Elspeth Willems

Another story—this time a vignette—based on "Beauty and the Beast." The original tale also has roots in much earlier depictions of unexpected compassion, such as that of Cupid and Psyche.

On the north side of town where the forest met the mountains, the Beast lived in his castle with Henry, the blacksmith's son. Henry was a red-haired young man with freckles dusted across his nose and cheeks, whose strength showed in the way he carried himself when he rode into the market every week to run errands for the Beast.

He bought meat from the butcher and vegetables, milk, and eggs from the farmers. Then he marched by his father, without even a glance, to buy flour and sugar.

When he was done, he walked his horse to the statue in the middle of the square where his childhood friend Annabel sat, her brown hair tied back with a blue ribbon and her hazel eyes focused on the lines in a book. He asked how she was doing now that her father was living in the city, thanks to one of his prize-winning inventions. She couldn't bring herself to move away from her home and the only person who understood her, even if it meant having Papa leave her behind.

"He sent a letter recently. A company bought his newest invention," she told Henry.

That's great, Belle," he said, but he pursed his lips as if he had heard all the words she hadn't spoken. Social stigma followed him like a cloud, but he wasn't the only victim. With Annabel's father away, she felt the stares of her neighbors much more intensely.

Henry's steps faltered as he turned to leave, his hands grasping the reins tighter than usual. It had been two years since he left his home against his parents' will to live in that castle. It weighed heavy on his heart, some days more than others.

"Henry," Annabel said, "how are you and Sebastian?"

His ears burned red at the sound of his partner's name—his *real* name. He turned to look at her, a sad smile playing at the edges of his lips. She was the only person who treated them fairly.

"Lonely. I've been talking to the tea cups." He laughed nervously. "Bash thinks we need a woman in the house to make it a home."

Annabel had known Sebastian before his parents passed away and before the fire. He was a burly young man with thick brown hair and dark, prominent features—and more recently, scars from burns that covered his left arm and extended up his shoulder, stopping just short of his neck. Despite his parents' wishes, he had refused to marry and have children, and when the townspeople caught wind, rumors spread: The words *queer* and *bigamist* were muttered in hushed tones like profanity. His parents' wealth and power protected him for a time, but when his father finally passed a year after his mother, the men came for Sebastian—a sinful beast in their eyes—with torches fueled by kerosene and hatred. Henry had been the only one to stand by his side, sword in hand, because he knew the feelings Sebastian had. Henry empathized in a way that no one else could—except perhaps Annabel, who kept her nose in a book and her feelings quietly to herself as she rejected one suitor after another.

"You should come into town more often," Annabel suggested, and Henry nodded absently.

"Thank you for caring, Annabel. I'll see you next week."

They could feel the glares of the marketgoers as Henry mounted his horse, a beautiful chestnut-colored French Trotter that whinnied when Annabel petted his muzzle. He belonged to Sebastian, one of a few Trotters that he had inherited from his parents, and while Henry took each to town in turn, Philippe was his favorite.

He rode back the way he came, disappearing into the thick of the woods as Philippe carried him north.

The next week, Henry rode into the market and dismounted his horse at the edge of the square, but today a second horse followed behind him, its rider wearing a cloak that covered most of his face. Henry kept one hand on his sword and reached for his partner with the other. Sebastian dropped his hood so that it draped his shoulders and allowed Henry to guide him through the maze of market stands and shocked bodies, their fingers interlaced as the crowd parted around them. The loud bustle quieted to hushed whispers of "the Beast."

Annabel looked up from her book and locked eyes with Henry. He marched straight ahead as he always did, but Sebastian trailed behind him, glancing anxiously back and forth, his jaw tense. He held both horses' reins like a lifeline, ready to mount his Trotter and escape at the first sign of violence.

Annabel dropped her book when she saw the man with her friend—the Beast who looked terrified of his own people, with scars they created from their ignorance and judgments.

That could have been me, she thought, but only Henry knew, and he had kept her secrets like he had kept Sebastian's, locked in the castle where they were safest. He used to hold her hand when they were alone. Seeing him with Sebastian now, she missed that feeling, but she understood that Sebastian needed him more than she did.

"Good morning, Belle," Henry said.

She stood, looking from one man to the other. Sebastian's dark eyes were a sharp contrast against the clear blue of Henry's. He watched her carefully, uncertain of her intentions but mesmerized by her beauty.

"Oh, Henry! Good morning." She smiled. "It's nice to see you, Sebastian."

Sebastian flinched at her words but seemed to soften when he heard his name.

"Annabel," he said quietly. "I haven't seen you in years."

She nearly collapsed under the weight of his words. Though he hadn't meant them to be accusatory, she felt sick to her stomach remembering the night the men had stormed through the woods to his home while she watched through her window. Henry had told her stay, and she was relieved when he did. Unlike Henry, she was afraid to swim against the current.

"I'm sorry," she said, though she knew it wasn't enough.

Henry waved off her apology. "We have something for you."

Sebastian's eyes darted nervously to the crowd glaring at him. Henry picked up the book that Annabel had dropped and opened it, flipping through the pages casually. As he closed it, he slipped an envelope between the hardcover and title page, then handed it back to her with a smile.

"We hope you'll accept," Sebastian said, making a clear effort to speak to her. He would have smiled had he not been so wary of the atmosphere, distinctly aware of the way the crowd was hissing the word "Beast" over and over, muttering speculations and defilements for simply stepping out of his isolated castle. He had hesitated to leave the privacy of those stone walls, even if only for a short time, but Henry wanted him to be there when he gave Annabel the invitation.

She looked curiously at the cover without opening it, strangely nervous about what Henry would give her to read only in private. "Thank you."

"I'll come back tomorrow. We can discuss it then," Henry said.

Annabel nodded. A sudden movement to her left caught her attention: An angry man trudged toward them. Before she could blink, Henry unsheathed his sword, pointing the tip directly at the man's chest, which stopped him in his tracks.

"Y-you're not welcome here, Beast!" the protester shouted nervously.

Sebastian pulled himself on to his horse's saddle, replacing his hood. "I can assure you, I do not plan on staying."

But as Annabel stepped in front of Henry, pushing the sword aside, Sebastian froze.

"Shame on you, Monsieur Bernard!" she scolded.

"A belle like you shouldn't be interacting with beasts like them." He hissed the last few words through clenched teeth, his gaze never wandering from Henry and Sebastian.

She clicked her tongue, mustering a confident tone that clashed with the knots in her stomach. "We happened to be having a lovely conversation before you so rudely interrupted. Go back to your shop. Leave these poor boys alone."

Monsieur Bernard blushed and turned to walk away, muttering under his breath. He wouldn't dare hurt a woman, and she knew it. Even with him gone, though, Sebastian stayed astride, his eyes locked on Annabel in a way that made her smile.

Henry put away his sword but kept a hand on the hilt. "You didn't have to do that."

She shrugged nonchalantly, grinning at him. "Well, I can't have you threatening to slice the entire town. Those odds are dangerously in your favor."

Henry laughed, his shoulders still tense.

"Thank you, Annabel," Sebastian said. "But I worry about you stepping in to our battle."

"It's the least I can do. Two years late though," she sighed.

"Better late than never. You're terrible with a sword anyway," Henry teased.

For the first time, Sebastian laughed, a soft rumble from his chest that made his shoulders relax and his abdomen tighten. It was one of Henry's favorite sounds, and he felt relieved to hear it here of all places. Unfortunately, the laughter was short-lived as the crowd began inching closer.

"We should get back to the castle," Sebastian said quickly.

Henry frowned, but he nodded and mounted his horse. "Tomorrow before sunrise? Under the oak tree near your house."

"I'll be there," she promised.

As soon as their horses began to gallop away, Annabel ran home clutching the book close to her chest until she reached the safety of her bedroom. Though she knew she was alone, she closed the curtains and sat against the back of the door. She opened the cover carefully, as if the letter might have vanished when she wasn't looking, but then unceremoniously ripped the edge of the envelope and shook out the contents. A single piece of monogrammed stationary fell to the wood floor, the crease in the middle keeping it folded. She slipped her fingers along the end to reveal handwriting she did not recognize. It was smaller and neater than Henry's, but he had signed his name at the bottom next to Sebastian's.

Dear Annabel, it read, *The honor of your presence is requested for dinner and dancing.*

It had no date or time written, simply the invitation with their signatures. Annabel tucked it into the center of the novel like a bookmark and placed it on her nightstand, feeling conflicted as she fought the butterflies filling her stomach.

Henry arrived before Annabel. He sat lazily under the oak tree, his sword lying on the grass beside him and his horse tied to a nearby fence. The sun still hadn't risen, but the sky began to color itself pink and orange.

Annabel came running, holding her shoes in one hand and the bottom of her dress with the other. When she rounded the tree, Henry stood to greet her.

"Hi," she huffed breathlessly.

Henry laughed quietly. "You didn't have to rush, Belle. I'm not in a hurry."

She hoisted herself on to the lowest tree branch and scooted along it to make room as Henry climbed up next to her. They swung their legs in mismatched time, the way they had when they were kids. This was far from the first morning they had spent watching the sunrise together.

For a while, they sat in near-silence, listening to the steady hum of insects buzzing. Henry brushed the side of his hand along Annabel's before lacing his fingers through hers.

"You read the invitation?" he finally asked, voice soft.

"Of course."

He smiled and shook his head. "I saw you run home with it yesterday. You're so eager sometimes, but others…I told Bash I wasn't sure if you would accept. I know you like to keep that part of you private. If we asked anyone, though, it had to be you."

"Why?" Hesitation crept up her spine, making her shiver.

"Because you understand his feelings better than even I do."

Annabel frowned. Henry knew, but he had always loved her anyway. He could have lived comfortably in one; instead, he chose Sebastian's. Even so, he had never strayed far from Annabel.

"Does Sebastian know that?"

"I told him, yes."

"Is that the only reason he invited me?"

Although she expected him to roll his eyes or tease her, Henry laughed and squeezed her hand. The warmth from his skin was comforting in the chill of the morning.

"No. I wanted you, and he understood. Besides, he finds you 'aesthetically pleasing.'" He leaned his shoulder against hers, and it reminded her of the day she had said that to him, desperately trying to put her incoherent thoughts into words.

"You want me to come to dinner?"

"Dinner…and whatever happens afterward."

"Henry," she chided.

"I'm not asking for anything you're not comfortable giving, Annabel. You know I wouldn't put you in that position, and Sebastian is like you. He isn't attracted to anyone in that way. Honestly, he wants the same as you do, but we've both been itching for another partner to love. You're the only person in town who knows what that feels like. We're just asking you to consider."

"Why did you choose us, of all people? You could have married a woman, had children with her, and lived normally in town—happily ever after."

"So could you. You have men practically lining up at your door, tripping over themselves to win your hand. You could marry one of them and force yourself to do things that you don't want to do, but you don't, because that's not who you are. And that's not who I am, either. Neither of us want that life. You and Sebastian are more important to me than a false sense of normalcy."

Henry sighed, and there was a long pause.

"But Annabel, you know if you accept our invitation—even just to dinner—the town won't see you as you anymore. *You will* be a beast to them, too. That's why Bash didn't write a date on the invitation. So you can think about what you want for as long as you need."

Suddenly, Annabel's chest felt tighter as she realized what he meant.

"You want me to live in the castle?"

"It's not as terrible as it sounds. Sebastian doesn't like to leave, but you and I could ride into town or walk through the woods. We could climb and explore like we used to, have dinner together, the three of us. Sebastian has an enormous library, too. It would be…I mean, if you want, it could be nice."

Sebastian and Henry locked themselves away from everyone else, but Annabel knew they were open and honest with each other—they acted like themselves because they didn't have anyone to force them otherwise. They enjoyed the solitude, a quiet life free of the judging eyes that followed them in town—something that Annabel had always craved. Though no one knew explicitly, her neighbors had always looked at her as if she were odd, and those unspoken words made her feel lonely without Henry by her side.

But what would happen if she and Sebastian didn't get along? They hadn't played together since they were children. He could be an entirely different person now. It felt risky to make a decision based on her emotions—but that was it. She hated that she worried what others thought of her, that she had to hide the way she felt, the way she *was*, because it wasn't standard. And here was Henry, happy simply to be himself with the people who loved him for it.

Annabel wanted to take that risk.

"Dinner and 'afterward' sound perfect," she said, and although she felt nervous, the confidence she heard in her voice seemed to convince her otherwise.

"Are you sure?" Henry asked quietly.

"The only thing I have ever been sure about is my trust in you, but I've always been a beast in their eyes. I might as well embrace it."

Henry smiled and kissed the back of her hand. The butterflies in Annabel's stomach settled to a calm excitement, determined to overcome the uneasiness that had always smothered her for being different.

"Then we'll live happily ever after," he declared. "The beauty and her beasts."

Glass Mountains
by Will Shughart

*This story is based on "The Black Bull of Norroway," a fairy
tale from Scotland retold in print since 1870.*

End to end of the horizon they stretched, black glass
shot through with bands of rainbow hue where the sunlight hit
their polished faces, translucent and razor sharp along their
jagged peaks. That was how the boy first saw them, emerging
from the tangle-wooded glen: like the raw, unfinished edge of
the world, warped by the fire that made it. A long time he
stood there, his shaded eyes scanning the fractured slopes, till
they caught the faintest glint of gold nestled between what
looked like two vast broken arrowheads.

That must be the place, he thought, the castle called East of the Sun and West of the Moon. That's where he'll be.

He shrugged his shoulders, shifting the too-light sack slung across them, and started across the endless empty plain.

●

"You don't have to go, Boots," Julianna had told him, breaking away from his embrace.

He sat up straighter against the stable wall to look down into her eyes, brushing a strand of hair out of her face. It was a vivid red, as her mother's must once have been to have gained the epithet by which the village knew her.

"Everyone goes to Auburn Mary," he said. "Both my sisters did, and look how well they've done."

"But you already know," Julianna insisted.

"Then she won't tell me who I'm to marry, will she? I'll find out what adventures I'm to have, or what sort of a man I'm to become, instead."

"And if she tells you different? That you're to marry someone else? Or to go away, and never come back?"

He kissed her reassuringly, held her closer. "I'll always come back to you."

It had the sound of a solemn promise.

The washerwoman's hut stood on the edge of a dark forest, far from the other houses. The curtains were drawn, and he saw it was dark inside as he tentatively pushed at the unlatched door.

"Hello?"

"Come in," said Auburn Mary. Her back was to him as he entered, her mass of white hair glinting in the low firelight as she rocked gently in her chair, but still she said at once: "Boots the stableboy, come to seek his fortune."

"I've brought you your bannock and your collop," he offered, voice high and quavering. Somehow he had never noticed that, even seated, she was much taller than he. He had never put much stock in the rumors that she was an ettin's daughter, if only because he could never believe Julianna was an ettin's granddaughter, but he wondered now.

She nodded and gestured to the empty chair beside her. "Leave them on the table, dear, and come sit." He obeyed. Still staring into the flames, she said: "When your eldest sister came to me, I sent her to watch at the back door. Two days she watched, and stayed with me nights, and on the third morning your brother-in-law came driving by in a coach-and-six. It was only a coach-and-four for your next sister, but she was happy enough, I know. What'll it be for you, I wonder?"

"Shall—shall I go to the back door, then?" he asked, hopefully. He knew who he would meet there on her way home.

She smiled, shook her head. "Oh no, dear, it's a different path for you. Long and difficult, I'm afraid. It's into the very heart of the forest you must go, to see what you can see."

●

With his first tentative step onto the first of the foothills, he knew it was impossible. The mountains were as slick as ice, and harder: too hard to chip away footholds with any tool at his disposal. Still he steadied himself as best he could with his walking stick and heaved himself up, slipped, and banged his knee. He tried again. He moved slowly and cautiously; he ran, half-leaping from crag to crag. But each time he found himself back at the bottom of the slope, breathless, bruised, bloodied. The top of the hill taunted him, just out of reach. Yet even if he achieved it, how many more peaks, and how much higher and steeper, lay beyond? He tried again.

●

Boots was thirteen nights camping in the dark forest before he saw anything. As he had left Auburn Mary's house, Julianna had caught up to him and given him a sack with some provisions. "Good luck," she'd said, and "Don't be too long." He'd thought the loaf of bread, the joint of meat, and the small flask would have long since given out, yet he found to his amazement that they never diminished. They were a constant reminder of her.

On the fourteenth morning he came upon a great raven locked in mortal struggle, a serpent coiled round it, fluttering its wings and cawing piteously. Hardly stopping to think, he picked up a fallen branch near at hand, beat the snake away, pinned its head down. It hissed and flexed its fangs at him, but the raven took its chance. Boots looked away as it finished the job.

The raven hopped onto his shoulder, cocked its head and croaked at him, then flew off. Boots took the hint and followed. It led him through dense undergrowth to a gnarled old tree at the edge of a clearing, where it settled at last with six of its brethren. He watched them, then lowered his gaze and froze. The open space was blotted out by a terrible shadow. It snorted, pawing the ground with a cloven hoof. He'd heard stories of the monstrous Black Bull, but had never believed them. Yet there it stood, its massive shoulder higher than his head, its forward-curving horns as long and sharp as lances, and its eyes—he had expected flames and fury, but there was something in its soft brown eyes that put him at his ease. It spoke in a lowing voice:

"For your kindness to my friend this day, I will give you a sight."

Boots hesitated. Julianna was waiting for him. He'd already been away much longer than he'd intended, and who knew how far the Black Bull would take him? He did not have to go, he knew. But without quite knowing why, he was suddenly and irrevocably certain that he wanted to. He nodded; the Bull knelt down on his forelimbs.

"Come up now on my back."

They traveled all that day together, over nine bens, and nine glens, and nine mountain moors. Boots told the Bull about his life in the village. The Bull told him he was once called Valemon, and served as a squire at a castle called East of the Sun and West of the Moon.

As the last of the daylight failed, he said, "My sister's house is just ahead. We'll rest there for tonight."

The Black Bull went alone to the stable and sent Boots to the front door. The sister welcomed Boots as if he were her own brother, fed him well, and showed him to a soft, warm bed.

In the morning as he prepared to set out again, she came to him and handed him a golden apple. "A parting gift," she said, and whispered its secrets to him, concluding with a piece of advice: "Be bold."

He stepped out the door, and the Black Bull was there, waiting for him. They traveled all that day together, over six bens, and six glens, and six mountain moors. Boots told him about Julianna: how he'd loved her as long as he could remember, but wasn't so sure anymore. The Bull told him there was a boy at the castle he'd felt the same way about, that it happened that way sometimes.

They came to his second sister's house. The Black Bull went to the stable, and his sister welcomed Boots inside, fed him, and showed him to a soft, warm bed. In the morning she handed him a silver-handled walking stick, whispered its secrets to him, and told him: "Be bold."

The Bull was waiting outside for him again. They traveled all that day together, over three bens, and three glens, and three mountain moors. Boots told him how confused he'd been when Auburn Mary sent him into the forest, but that it was starting to make sense to him now. The Bull told him he'd been wandering the earth a long time, since the day his father called down a curse upon him, but he'd never met anyone he'd been as sure of as Boots.

They came to his third sister's house. The Black Bull went to the stable, and his sister welcomed Boots inside, fed him, and showed him to a soft, warm bed. In the morning she handed him a black velvet spangled cloak, whispered its secrets to him, and told him: "Be not too bold."

Standing outside was the handsomest boy he ever saw, beaming, with gold rings in his hair. There were bits of straw stuck in it, stuck to his skin. He was wearing nothing else.

"Have you seen a black bull?" Boots asked, looking into his soft brown eyes.

The boy said, "You'll never see the Black Bull again, for I am that bull. I was put under spells; it was meeting you that loosed me."

●

A distant clinking sound caught his ear as he walked along the plain, searching vainly for a pass. It echoed eerily in the silence of the shadow of the glass mountains, and he could not tell from what direction it came. Yet it grew steadily louder, and at last, rounding a crystal hummock, a low brick building came into view.

The door of the forge stood wide open, and within he could see the huge ettin smith at his anvil. He was afraid; he did not know whether to go forward or back; the ettin stayed his hammer and looked up.

"You'll be seeking a way through the mountains." His voice was the gentle rumbling of distant thunder. The boy nodded.

"I can make you shoes that will grip the glass, if you can pay."

He tossed his sack to the ettin's feet. "It's all I have," he said, for this was not yet the hour to spend his other gifts.

The ettin stooped and stretched the sack open with two massive fingers, examining its contents. He took huge bites from the meat and bread, watched them grow whole again; he took a swig from the flask that should have drained it nine times over, and found it full still.

"I will take this," he said.

The boy sighed in relief.

"But it is not enough. You'll have to work for the rest." He took up the red-hot iron and slammed the hammer down again. The sparks flew.

●

The sky was overcast as they set out on the last stretch of their journey, Valemon clad now in the armor his youngest sister had kept for him. He was walking a little ahead, where the ground sloped gently down toward a tangle-wooded glen, when he stopped abruptly in his tracks. Boots bumped into him and started to apologize when he saw the look of terror on his face.

"What is it?"

"The Old One is here," said Valemon. He loosened his sword in its scabbard, pointed out a flat gray rock jutting from the green hillside. "Stay there."

"Let me come with you," Boots pleaded, though he did not understand. "Let me help."

Valemon shook his head, spoke with finality. "I must face this alone. Wait for me—there, on that rock, and not one step away from it. If you move, if the Old One senses you, we'll never find each other again."

Boots sat reluctantly. Valemon kissed him, lingered, then turned away and started down the hill.

"How will I know?" Boots called out, his voice breaking.

He paused, looked over his shoulder. "If the sky turns blue, then I'll have prevailed. If it turns red—my sisters will look after you and see you safely home."

Boots waited anxiously for what seemed like hours, peering into the impenetrable wood, the inscrutable sky. Were those thunderclouds on the horizon? He fidgeted but did not move from his seat. They drifted closer, loomed overhead; they flickered with red lightning. The thunder boomed and Boots jumped up, half startled, half determined to rush to Valemon's aid.

The sky was blue and cloudless. Boots ran down into the glen, calling Valemon's name. But all was still and quiet. There was not a living thing to be found.

●

Seven years he had labored for the ettin smith. Now he strapped on heavy boots with sharp iron nails in the soles, and he clutched a map that showed the way to the castle. The parchment was ancient, the ink faded: the ettin had found it at the bottom of a trunk beneath whole atlases of latter ages whose cartographers had forgotten there ever were glass mountains. He took his first tentative step onto the first of the foothills. The nails scraped the surface, then bit, and held.

Between the arrowhead peaks stretched a green meadow, the first he had seen since that day in the tangle-wooded glen. The castle's golden turrets glimmered in the distance, not a short walk, but an easy one after his arduous climb. Nearer at hand a patch of brown, a movement caught his eye: a strangely familiar hut stood on the grounds, and before it a figure in travel-worn clothes was engaged in some frantic activity. As he drew closer, he saw she had an old gray shirt, stained with rust-colored blotches, that she was dipping into a bucket of suds then scrubbing on a washboard. Back and forth, faster and harder, but while her hands grew redder and rawer, the shirt never got any cleaner. He bent to take it from her, to offer to help.

The shirt was white. The girl looked up, her eyes wide with surprise.

"Boots?" she said.

"Julianna?"

●

Reunited at the edge of the world, Boots told Julianna of his long journey into the glass mountains, and Julianna told Boots how Auburn Mary had sent her there. She'd heard that a knight had returned from a long absence to the castle East of the Sun and West of the Moon. He'd pledged to marry whomsoever could wash the bloodstains from his shirt, and many had tried and failed, but Mary said it was a task a washerwoman's and sorceress's daughter was made for.

"So I walked across the deep night sky to come here. The Sun told me that I once had seven brothers; the Moon told me Auburn Mary cursed them when I was born, for they tarried too long fetching water for my baptism; and the Stars told me they had seen them now and again as ravens, flying over the glass mountains.

I never cared about marrying a knight, but I thought if I did this thing he might tell me where to find them, how to save them."

"Well, and you've done it," said Boots, handing her the unspotted garment.

"Have I?" she wondered.

"Still I'd like to see this knight for myself before you wed him, if I might."

"No one sees him during the day. They say he goes out hunting. But he retires to a chamber in the castle at sundown."

"Will you let me go in to him, then?"

She smiled. "What'll you give me for it?"

He thought a moment, then took the cloak from his shoulders. "Wrap this all around yourself and you'll be invisible: you can slip into the castle unnoticed to search for some sign of your brothers."

"Thank you," she muttered as she took it, eyes downcast. "I—I thought you might offer me something else."

"I would have, once," he told her, gently squeezing her hand. "A part of me would still, and gladly. But after all, it's very different roads we've walked to come here."

The castle gates stood open. Boots crossed the threshold's paving stones inlaid with fiery letters that spelled: Be bold. The entrance hall was vast and hung with tapestries of Jove in his many shapes: a storm and shower, a swan and bull. He saw an eagle flying off with a girl; he saw an eagle flying off with a boy. At the end was a statue of a beautiful golden youth, winged with rainbow pinions, blindfolded and wielding a bow, standing in triumph atop a dragon pierced with arrows. He circled round, examining it. Behind was an iron door, and on the lintel were engraved the words: Be bold.

The second hall was smaller, paneled all in gold, chased with strange moving figures he dared not linger on. And there were seven iron doors, all inscribed with that same motto: Be bold. But no, he realized, looking closer, there was one with different words: Be not too bold. He hesitated before it, then ignored its warning and pushed.

There was Valemon in his bed, handsome as ever, eyes closed, chest slowly rising and falling. Boots whispered his name, then said it louder. He nudged him gently, then shook him. He cried out for him to wake, but he would not—could not. Something was wrong. He tried again.

He waited; he tried again; he fought off sleep as long as he could. He thought he closed his eyes for a moment, and it was morning, and Valemon had vanished.

Back down at the washerwoman's hut, he told Julianna what had happened.

"I'm sorry," she said.

"And how did you fare?"

"There's a door in the glass in the bottom of the deepest dungeon. I tried everything I could, and it wouldn't open. I think it's there they'll be."

He held out his walking stick. "Knock three times with this, and any door will open. Give me another night with him and it's yours."

She nodded. "It's a deal."

But it was the same story he had to tell her the next morning.

"I'm sorry," she said.

"And you?"

"Behind the door is a glass cave, and in the cave a glass table laid with seven empty crystal plates and seven empty crystal cups. But no one was there and no one came, though I waited."

Boots reached into his trousers pocket and produced his golden apple. "I don't know what use you'll find for this," he admitted. "Only I was told to save it for my hour of greatest need."

"One more night," Julianna agreed, taking the apple. "Then I'm bringing him the shirt. Good luck."

That evening he passed through the halls once more, and came to the bedchamber. His heart leapt when he saw the iron door was ajar. He hurried in.

Valemon stood facing the window, and did not turn as Boots entered, but cocked his ear and spoke with a smile in his voice.

"Seven ravens dwell inside this mountain, old friends of mine, robbed of their proper shapes and voices. A golden apple appeared on their table. No one saw who put it there, but they were hungry and devoured it, core and all. Inside was a golden ring inscribed with the true name of Auburn Mary. That was the object that cursed them; that restored them to their former selves. Earlier this evening one came and told me he's been hearing a voice for the past two nights. From this room. A familiar voice, he said. Someone who saved his life once.

"I always have a glass of wine before bed. Tonight I skipped it, for which I think Auburn Mary, with her spells and potions, won't thank me. But you—"

He turned at last, and at the look in his eyes Boots rushed into his waiting arms.

"I've been looking for you, too," Valemon said. "Every day."

●

"You don't have to go," he'd told her. "There's more than enough room in the castle for all of us." But Julianna had shaken her head and smiled.

"I'll leave you to it. My brothers want to get away and I'm going with them, for now. After that, who knows? I'm going to seek my fortune."

Now it was just the two of them. Valemon offered Boots his hand.

"I believe I promised you a sight," he said.

And hand in hand they climbed the winding stair to the top of the tallest tower. Arm in arm they walked to the golden parapet.

Boots gasped when he saw it. They stood, just looking and holding one another, for a long time before he could think of anything to say.

"They're beautiful from here," he whispered at last.

Glittering glass mountains, as far as the eye could see.

Brenna
by Emmy Clarke

This story is a version of "Ferdinand the Faithful and Ferdinand the Unfaithful," another German fairy tale collected by the Brothers Grimm.

As a child, Brenna lived in a small, lonely house atop a hill with her wise old godmother. Though they were not wealthy, Brenna and her godmother felt very rich of heart. They loved each other dearly, and there was never a day that passed without them saying so.

When Brenna was seven, her godmother presented her with a gift. The gift came in a red velvet pouch, and it was the first that Brenna had ever received. She opened the pouch with shaking hands, too excited even to breathe. Within it lay a tiny golden key.

"On your fourteenth birthday," said Brenna's godmother, "a castle will appear in the meadow below our house. This key will unlock the castle doors, and whatever you find inside will be yours to keep."

Brenna was so excited she rushed down to the meadow at once. But of course the castle was not there, and would not appear for seven more years.

And so Brenna was patient.

On the morning of her fourteenth birthday, Brenna's godmother would not wake up. She had died in the night. Unable to bear the sight, Brenna's eyes filled with tears. She fled from the house and went tearing down to the meadow, and there she was met by the sight of a magnificent golden castle.

Her hands went to her neck, where the velvet pouch was tied, and very carefully withdrew the key. In moments the key was in the lock; she turned it and heard a gentle click, and the door opened.

Within the main hall was a horse so beautiful Brenna could not take her eyes from it. The hall itself was tremendously grand, teeming with all sorts of dazzling decorations and fabulous furniture, but to her, the horse was more perfect and precious than any jewel. It was a black mare with dark brown eyes and a mane so soft it practically begged Brenna's fingers to run through it.

For a moment Brenna forgot her sorrows. She led the mare from the castle and locked the door. She then hopped onto the mare's back and, without needing to tug at the reins—indeed, there weren't any reins to tug!—she persuaded the mare to take her uphill towards the house she had shared with her godmother. Once there, she went upstairs and into her godmother's room.

"Godmother," Brenna said, taking the old woman's cold, lifeless hand. "I am going on a journey."

Her godmother's voice seemed to echo in her mind, so clear it made Brenna let loose a gasp.

"Are you indeed?" said the voice in an amused tone. "Then you must keep the key to the castle with you at all times, and promise me that the first person you meet, you will ask them to travel by your side."

When alive, Brenna's godmother had always seemed to know things others did not. Brenna knew that her godmother would never steer her wrong, and so she made a solemn promise to accept the guidance of whomever she met along the road. Then she gave her godmother a kiss on the forehead and set off on her journey.

As they went down the road, Brenna spoke to the mare of the life she had left behind. Though the mare remained silent, it seemed she listened to every word Brenna said, and often Brenna would lean forward and wrap her arms about her new friend's neck to convey how grateful she was for the mare's presence.

They did not get far before they met a girl on a white horse. The girl looked so familiar it unnerved Brenna, for having lived her whole life atop a hill she did not know very many people. But she remembered her godmother's words, and she asked the girl's name.

"Brenna," said the girl.

And here Brenna's knees went weak, and she would likely have toppled had her mare not snorted quite loudly, bringing her awareness back to her body. Brenna now realised why the girl looked so familiar. The girl on the white horse was Brenna's double. Why, they could have been twins!

Brenna did not want to travel alongside the girl on the white horse, but she could not bring herself to disobey her godmother's instructions. The girl on the white horse, however, was delighted to join her, and together they traveled to an inn.

Once there, Brenna soon became aware that her new companion was not the nicest of people. The Other Brenna drank heavily and yelled insults at men twice her size, and many times Brenna caught her stealing money from their pockets.

Brenna did not want to stand by and let her double commit crimes—especially not considering they shared a face! And yet, she did not want to report the Other Brenna's misdeeds, for then she would have to continue her journey alone, against her godmother's wishes.

So she went to the stables and talked to her friend, the mare, of her troubles.

"You must take your double and head to the king's palace," said the mare, much to Brenna's surprise. She concluded that horse must be magical, just like the castle. "There your problems shall come to an end."

Now, Brenna wasn't about to argue with a talking horse. She hurried back indoors and pulled the Other Brenna away from the bar, and together they climbed upon their horses and rode to the palace. The Other Brenna was too intoxicated to ask questions.

As they approached the palace, a member of the royal guard stopped them.

"Are you here to offer your services?" he asked. "Are you here to save the queen?"

Brenna saw immediately that she must say yes, though she had no idea what had befallen the queen that she should need saving. The guard brought them to the king, who was lamenting—rather noisily—in his throne room.

"Here!" said the Other Brenna loudly, finally realising where she was. "That's the bloody king!"

The king was too absorbed in his own misery to notice her rudeness. "You are here to rescue the queen?" he asked.

Brenna thought it wise to be honest. "Actually, Your Highness, we were just passing through. But we would be happy and proud to help rescue the queen, if only we knew what has happened to her."

"Today marks the seventh anniversary of my wife's abduction," said the king, after blowing his nose on his sleeve. "She was stolen from me, along with my daughter, by the wickedest of wizards. He killed my daughter and gave my wife to the water giants of the west!"

"Goodness!" Brenna cried. "How terrible!"

"Surely your wife is dead by now," said the Other Brenna heartlessly. "If it has been seven years, the water giants must have eaten her."

"Not so!" said the king. "She lives still. Every evening, I go to the cliff overlooking the sea and listen to her sing. I would know her voice anywhere. She is alive!"

Brenna's eyes brimmed with tears. "Then we will bring her back. When does the rescue party leave, and on which ship?"

"Rescue party?" said the king. "There is no rescue party. I sent my entire army to war with the giants years ago, and they were defeated one and all. The water giants sank their ships and gobbled them up. If you agree to go, I shall send you out on a fishing boat tomorrow morning."

"And what if we don't agree?" said the Other Brenna.

"Then I shall execute you for wasting royal time," said the king gravely.

"Royal time!" the Other Brenna scoffed, but Brenna silenced her by placing a hand over her mouth.

"We'll go," she said. "We'd be glad to help."

The king gave the two girls rooms in his palace, and placed guards by their doors. The guards were exceedingly polite, for if the girls had not agreed to face the water giants, then one of them would have been sent instead. They did not hesitate to explain to Brenna that she had, in effect, sentenced herself to death.

Brenna did not feel much like sleeping that night. Every hour, she opened her door a crack and peeked through, and when she saw that her guard had nodded off, she scurried out of her room. She dashed down to the palace stables, where she fell weeping by her mare's hooves.

"What have I done?" she sobbed. "I can't fight water giants—I have never fought anything larger than a spider!"

"You will not have to fight them," said the mare.

Brenna looked up at her friend, hardly daring to believe her ears.

"You see," the mare continued, "water giants are simple creatures. They seem cruel on the outside, but in truth all they desire is to be shown respect. Sneak into the palace kitchen and take as much raw meat as you can fit in a sack. When you encounter the giants, throw the meat to them and announce that you have come to parley. They will not harm you. They do not like to harm others, or they would have killed the queen as soon as they saw her."

Brenna saw the sense in this.

"But I don't want to steal from the king," she said.

"You won't be," said the mare. "I cannot explain yet, but I will. Go now, be swift!"

And so, Brenna returned to the palace. She snuck into the kitchen and filled a sack with raw meat, then scurried back to her room to wait for dawn to break.

The next morning, as they boarded the tiny fishing boat, the Other Brenna was oddly silent. She did not speak to Brenna for a long while, and when she did they were far, far from land. Her tone was dangerous.

"What's the bag for, Brenna?"

"Nothing," Brenna said, too quickly.

"You're lying," said her double. "Give it here."

Trapped in the small boat, Brenna had no choice but to hand over the sack.

"Meat!" the Other Brenna declared, pulling out a hunk of something-or-other and waving it in front of Brenna's face. "What for?"

Brenna shrugged. "Dinner."

"Oh?" The Other Brenna smiled knowingly. "Then you won't mind if I eat it." She did not wait for an answer but began chomping away, cramming mouthful after mouthful of the raw, stinking meat past her lips.

Brenna watched in horror.

"Delicious!" the Other Brenna declared. "Want some?"

Brenna shook her head. She felt sick. She would have leapt into the water had she known how to swim. But as it was, there was no escape—and how was she to parley with the water giants now? In the space of a few minutes, the Other Brenna had eaten all the raw meat.

Just then, there was a loud blast of sound as something burst out of the water behind them. A water giant rose higher and higher into the air, and the smell of salt stung Brenna's nose and eyes. She tilted back her head.

"What is this?" the water giant said, looming over them but leaning down, down, down to get a closer look.

The Other Brenna screamed and punched him in the eye.

For a moment nothing happened. And then the water giant roared, snatched the Other Brenna up in one huge fist and dropped her into his wide, gaping mouth. He swallowed her whole.

Brenna stared at him, terrified that he would eat her up, too, for the Other Brenna's rudeness came from a face that looked much like her own. Then she gathered herself up and called up to him, "I am sorry for her rudeness, Sir!"

The water giant peered down at her. "What's hers is not yours, my dear, however alike you may look. Why are you here?"

"I'm here on behalf of the king," Brenna said, gaining courage. "I am here to parley."

The giant nodded. The gesture dislodged a large fish from his nostril; it plummeted into the water, and the resulting splash drenched Brenna from head to toe.

"He wants his queen back, I assume," said the giant. "Well, he can have her. We grew bored of her years ago, you know."

He descended back underwater and mere seconds later a head rose up above the waves. It was the head of an extremely pretty woman with a dainty, shining crown set amongst her dark curls.

Brenna helped the queen aboard the boat, and together they made their way back to shore.

Upon their return, the king howled with glee and wrapped his queen in his cloak to keep her from shivering. Then he shook Brenna's hand far more vigorously than was necessary and called for a feast to be prepared at once.

Brenna's mare was there to meet her. Brenna hugged her friend, sliding her fingers through the mare's soft, silky mane.

"And now," said the mare, "I have something to show you, Brenna."

Breaking free of Brenna's grip the mare did three full runs round the palace, and when she was finished, she threw back her head and transformed into a beautiful young girl.

The king began to cry. "My daughter! My beautiful daughter!"

The princess went to her father and squeezed his hand. "It's good to see you again, papa."

"But how—how?" he spluttered.

"When the wizard took us, he transformed me into a horse and locked me in a hidden castle. He sent mama to the water giants, and cast a spell so that even if I were found, I would be unable to change back if mama was still at sea."

"Why didn't you tell someone?" said the king. "Why didn't you tell me at once?"

"The wizard was cunning," said the princess. "He crafted his spell so that I would be unable to tell anyone of its depth. I couldn't breathe a word of it! Unfortunately for him, Brenna's wise old godmother, a powerful good witch, was watching him. Before he could leave the hidden castle, she swept in to confront him.

"The wizard, knowing of the witch's love for her godchild, cursed Brenna to be split in two. Brenna retained her good heart, yet her double had no heart at all, and existed solely to torment the old woman. Still, Brenna's godmother defeated the wizard and sealed him inside a grain of sand. She could reverse neither spell nor curse, but she vowed that in seven years, when the spell had weakened, someone would come to my aid. Seven years passed—Brenna came. She saved me. She saved us both!"

The princess glided towards Brenna, took her hand, and kissed it. Brenna blushed.

"You still have the key to your castle, don't you?" asked the princess.

Brenna nodded. Of course she did, her godmother had told her never to part with it!

"Then let us go," said the princess with a wink. "I should like to see it again."

"Well," said Brenna, "I should like to join in the feast first!"

And so, after much hearty feasting, Brenna and her princess rode off on the white horse, and they lived together in Brenna's golden castle for many, many years.

The Last Lost Boy
by George Lester

A retelling of "Peter and Wendy," more commonly known as "Peter Pan," by Scottish novelist and playwright J. M. Barrie.

Bright eyes burn from the open window. The light of the moon hits the side of a boy's face, but mostly keeps him in shadow as he perches on my window ledge and stares inside. He doesn't move. He just sits there, like he's waiting for something, looking for someone. Maybe he's lost.

How he even got up here is beyond me. We're on the second floor, for goodness sake. Downstairs, people are *still* at the party, dancing, singing, screeching. I can feel the bass through the floor, the music pulsing through the house and into my veins, keeping me awake.

Will Mum even be able to drive me tomorrow?

Everything is packed. The car loaded up and fit to burst. I had gone to bed at a decent hour so I could at least attempt to make a good impression.

Will she ask me to drive? I've never done a motorway before.

The shadow shuffles around, and I stiffen. Even if I call out, no one would hear me. This is it. This is the end.

Just.

Stay.

Still.

"Hey stranger!" the voice of the boy hisses into the room and I flinch. I know I flinch. It could've been seen from space, even in the dark. "Big day tomorrow, huh?"

I recognize the voice. I can't quite place it—the way he has lowered it to stay quiet is making it hard—but there is a sing-song quality to it, a lilt that stirs memories. "Look, I saw you packing the car and I wanted to say goodbye, but I hadn't seen you in so long, I didn't think you'd want to see *me*, and I'm sorry for climbing up to your window but—"

"Peter?" The words slip from my mouth before I have a chance to stop them, more of a gasp than anything else. What on earth was Peter Ansell doing in my house?

"I wasn't sure you'd remember—"

"You vanished." And my words are so blunt that I swear the party downstairs grinds to a halt.

Peter shifts. I sit up, keeping the covers over my very naked bottom half but letting the cool night air hit my chest. Damn, it's hot.

"You grew up," he says softly. I look down, the silvery light streams in from the window and lights me up. I look ghostly.

"Of course I did," I whisper. "It's been ten years, it was bound to happen."

Peter chuckles in the dark; I can see the movement, hear the throaty noise. I want to flick my lamp on, see if he's still the same redheaded boy I spent so much of my childhood with.

"Peter, why are you here?"

I hear him hesitate.

"Mum brought me back. Nana isn't well."

I remember Nana. He loves his Nana.

"But I saw you getting ready to leave, and I hadn't realized, and I nearly came over earlier but didn't think you'd want to see me."

"I would have."

"What?"

"I would have wanted to see you."

"Oh."

It seems so simple. I can't imagine a time where I wouldn't want to see Peter Ansell. Maybe just after he'd left. He didn't say goodbye.

"Where did you go?" I say to the dark.

"Everything fell apart with Mum and Dad, so Mum packed up and took me away with her."

"I wish you'd said goodbye."

"I wish I had too." I hear him sigh, and he stands.

"Are you going again?" I move around on the bed, flinging my legs over the side as if I'm about to go and stop him, which just seems absurd.

"I don't..." he trails off. "What's happening downstairs?"

"Leaving party."

"For you?"

"Yep."

"Why are you up here?" He laughs through the words, and it sounds like the old Peter but deeper and it is everything. It's like I'm eight again.

"I wanted to sleep before tomorrow," I sigh. "Gotta go to Uni, meet people I'll be living with for the next year, try and convince them I'm not completely socially inept."

"You're not."

"You've not seen me in ten years, maybe I am."

"I *know* you're not." I almost believe him. It's enough to put a smile on my face, at least.

He crosses to the window and I see his silhouette in full. He is tall now, broad-shouldered and just a whole lot bigger than the gangly eight year old I knew. He grew up too. We grew up without each other, and considering how close we used to be, it just doesn't seem quite right.

"How did you get up here?" I say.

I hear him smile. "Get dressed and I'll show you."

I almost tell him to shove it but there is a mischief in his eyes, a dare, like he remembers the me from ten years ago and knows that I'm probably too chicken.

I grab my boxers and jeans, diving under the bed sheets and pulling them on. My t-shirt is hanging on the back of my desk chair, so I put it on, slipping on a pair of Vans and find myself standing right next to Peter.

He's really grown up; I can see it in his face. Though his eyes still have that boyish spark, that burning joy, his jaw has become more defined, a smattering of fuzz across a jawline so sharp it could cut me. He still has his freckles, a constellation across his nose and cheeks.

"Well, would you look at that," he says softly, grinning.

"What?"

He pulls the window open as wide as it will go and starts out of it.

"You can follow if you want," he says, the grin so wide it practically splits his face. "One last adventure. For old time's sake. What do you think?"

"I think I might fall."

"It's all part of the excitement." He grins. "Come on, Will. One more night?"

And then he's gone. I lean out of the window and there he is, shimmying down the drainpipe, using the vines and gaps in the brickwork as foot and hand holds. I suddenly feel like I can't do it. My stomach is performing a floor routine.

"Come on," he hisses up, nearly at the bottom. "It's not that far when you get going, just try not to look down."

"How will I see where I'm going?"

"You'll just have to trust me," he says. "Don't make that face, just trust me."

I haul my body out of the window, feeling heavier than I did a few seconds ago. I lower myself, my legs dangling, kicking about at the brickwork, scuffing my shoes and trying to find a foothold.

"A little to the left!" Peter calls up.

Shifting myself and swinging my legs left, I find a place to shove the toe of my shoe. It seems stable so I lean on it, finding another just a little way below.

I steady myself on the drainpipe, hearing it creak, feeling it move, knowing it couldn't possibly support my entire weight. I keep going, foothold after handhold after drainpipe after vine, making my way down the side of my own house and wondering what anyone would think if they saw me now.

"Just let go!" he hisses up at me. I look down, the exact thing he told me not to do, but I'm not that far off the ground. One deep breath. I drop and feel him grab me, steadying me as I reach the ground.

I find myself staring up into his eyes, his arms wrapped tightly around my waist. He is grinning down at me. He really has grown up.

"Where to now?" I say softly, wondering if he can hear me over the pulsing bass coming from the party.

Peter releases my waist and grabs hold of my hand, running me to the end of my garden and through a gap in the fence. I don't blink; I don't get a chance to think about it, because Peter Ansell is leading me off into the night.

The night is warm, and I have no idea where we're going. His hand is gripping me so tightly I can feel the sweat pooling between our palms. We dart across a road, a car blaring its horn as we pass in front of it. The lights blind me. I realize, as we draw to a halt on the pavement, that I'm laughing, laughing so hard that my cheeks hurt, laughing so hard that I can hardly breathe, bent double, leaning against a wall for support.

"What are you playing at?" I gasp.

"We were running," he pants. "We've got places to be, Will, we can't afford to be late."

"Oh can't we?"

"Not at all!" He leans back against the wall with me, our arms touching, the warmth coming off him in waves. "Ready?"

I look up at him. The streetlamp above makes the sheen of sweat on his face shine. That grin. That grin that is plastered across his face, one side of it a little higher than the other, his two front teeth crossing over a little, his eyes on fire.

"Of course."

He grabs hold of my hand again and drags me back onto the pavement, past people who shout after us because we're going too fast, faster than my legs can really carry me, so fast it almost feels like flying.

We cross through the churchyard, the bells striking, telling me how late it is and that I should definitely still be in bed, but I can hardly hear them over the blood pumping in my ears, the joy rushing through my body.

The orange streetlamps fade as we move out of town and down a side street. I know this place. I have been to this place many times, but not recently. We stop outside the swimming pool and I try to catch my breath.

There is music. I can hear it. That same noise of bass pumping that had been at my house and I wonder for the briefest of moments if it is somehow carrying all the way from there to here. But it's coming from inside, accompanied by voices that laugh and talk and scream and sing out into the night.

"What are we doing here?" I pant.

"Party," he manages. "Everyone is about to go and grow up, so it's one last party. One more night, one more get together, before everyone goes and gets lost." He manages to catch his breath and stands up straight. I'm once again struck by how tall he is.

"I-I'm not invited," I stammer.

"I'm inviting you."

"You're sure."

"Will." He raises an eyebrow at me. "You know these people. They'll be glad to see you."

He takes hold of my hand again, lacing his fingers between mine, and I don't let myself question what it means when he keeps on doing this. It's just friendly. We're just friends. But this time we walk, we don't run. We walk around the side of the building, hand in hand, flickering fluorescent bulbs lighting our way and casting cruel shadows.

The noise increases as we get closer and I feel a hand close tightly over my chest. "From one party to another," I say softly.

Peter scoffs. "Hardly."

"Huh?"

"You weren't even at that party." He smiles. "You were hiding in your room."

"Trying to get a decent night's sleep—"

"While everyone down there, your family, wanted to wish you well as they sent you on your way into adulthood." We stop outside a fire exit, the side of his face bathed in a wash of green. "Was it an Annabel special?"

"It started that way," I say, surprised that he remembers my other mother and her parties. "But Mum got her hands on it and reigned her in a bit. You know what she's like."

"I remember, yeah," he sighs. "How are Mrs and Mrs Darling, then? I miss them."

"You do?"

"It was like I had four parents."

"They'd like that, you know," I say. "Oh, God, Peter, why did you have to leave? We've missed out on so much."

"I know."

He's still holding my hand.

"Growing up together, awkward gawky teen Will, you missed it! It's like a whole section of my life is missing because you weren't in it."

"That's a bit much."

I shrug. "It's true, though. It was weird when you left."

"I'm here now." He closes the gap between us and I feel my breath quicken. He leans forward, his forehead pressed against mine, his breath hot on my face and he's let go of my hand so he can place both his hands on my hips instead. I follow his lead like I have done all evening and hold him there too. I'm tingly, alive with feeling and color.

"Oh, Will," he breathes, so softly that it sounds more like a song than a name.

The door next to us swings outwards, clanging against the wall behind it. We're apart before I have a chance to think, though I don't know if it's he or I that pushes away. The music rushes out to meet us in a wave.

A girl is standing in the doorway, lit from behind by an unforgiving strip light, her dark hair wet at the tips and her even darker eyes glaring at us stood here in the alleyway. She readjusts her towel.

"Peter!" she shouts. "I knew it!"

"Who is it?" a voice calls from inside.

"It's Peter!" she calls back. "I told you!" She turns back to face us, beckoning us forward. As Peter reaches her, she throws her arms around him. "You're here!" She looks to me now. "And you brought a friend?"

"Yeah, this is—"

"Will, I know Will, we had Statistics together. Didn't know you were coming!" She hugs me, too. I realize how damp she is and try to pull her name from somewhere in the back of my head.

"Now quick, get inside," she says. "We're not exactly running a covert operation but we want to enjoy this as much as we can."

We step inside and she slams the door behind us, just in case the music hadn't already woken up half the neighborhood. We're led down a long corridor, the scent of chlorine permeating the air. It makes everything warm. The air is so thick I swim through it.

As we reach poolside, I see the party is in full swing. To one side, an iPhone has been hooked up to speakers, and near that is a table covered in bottles upon bottles of spirits and beers and stacks of solo cups. In and around the pool, faces I vaguely recognize drink and talk and dance and kiss and splash around. I breathe it in.

Don't panic.

Peter nudges me. "Glad you came?"

"Glad I nearly killed myself climbing out of my bedroom window to spend the evening with you?" I grin. "Yeah, a little."

"Peter!"

"Ah, jeez, it's Peter!"

The voices come in various combinations, shouting over one another as everyone welcomes Peter to the party, everyone pleased to see him.

"Izzy," Peter says to the girl. Isobel. That's her name. "Changing rooms?"

She points off to the other end of the pool. Peter grabs my hand again. The two of us walk the length of the pool to the changing rooms. They smell worse than the pool, damp with hints of leftover chlorine and cleaning product. I gag.

"I have no shorts," I say flatly.

He snorts and shakes his head. "Neither do I." He strips off his shirt, then his shoes, then his trousers, and he is stood in front of me in his boxer shorts and I honestly don't know where to look. "Your turn." He winks and I die.

"I don't know if—"

"Will, come on," Peter groans, closing that gap between us again. I can smell him. Boyish, a bit sweaty from the run, some aftershave that I feel like I recognize but probably don't. "Let's participate. One last night." He kisses me lightly, a kiss so light it was like a breeze tracing across my lips. "One. Last. Night."

Heat breaks across my body, my heart beating so fast it feels more like a hum. Suddenly brave, I pull my shirt over my head, kicking off my shoes and jeans until I'm standing in my boxer shorts. I feel embarrassed and empowered at the same time. Utterly thrilled and completely self-conscious. The feeling makes my chest hurt.

I gather my clothes and head out to the pool with him, putting them down in a messy pile to one side next to his. I'm standing in my local swimming pool, in my Union Jack underpants, and I could not feel more cold if I tried. Though I'm definitely sweating. Why is my body such a freaking war zone?

There are whoops and cheers. I suppress a grin as almost everyone, boy and girl, catcalls Peter for being there in his underwear. He looks good; I can't deny that he looks good. He's tall and broad and fit in a way that suggests playtime never ended for him. It's just normal, natural, broad shoulders, a smattering of freckles on his torso that you can see between light hairs.

"Come on, Peter, we've been waiting for you!" someone shouts. I can't quite tell who, but it makes me laugh. Until it doesn't.

And it dawns on me, suddenly, what has happened here. They were expecting him. *I* wasn't expecting him, but a dozen people who I have been at school with my whole life were.

"How did they know you were coming?" I asked.

He shrugs, stretching up into the air. "We stayed in touch."

"So you kept in touch with all these people?" I try and stay calm, try and not make it obvious that this hurts.

"A text here, a message there, sure, most of us are still in touch." He shrugs it off again and I burn.

"But not me." I see his face drop, and I feel myself getting teary-eyed. I blink it away. Now isn't the time, not with people here, not in front of everyone because they'll all look and I'll feel even more hot and embarrassed even though I'm not wearing a shirt and—

Peter's hands fall on my shoulders. "Please don't be upset," he whispers.

"How can I not be?" I keep my voice as even as I can, though a slight wobble betrays me. "People we went to primary school with, that now go to my secondary school, which you never even came to, know you, know who you are, where you've been, and I'm supposed to not be upset?"

"Will—"

"You were my best friend." Now I *am* crying, so I turn away from the pool and try to ignore the feeling of eyes on my back. "I wanted to call you but I didn't know where you were, I couldn't track you down online. You just vanished." Now it was Peter's turn to look hurt, but I kept going. "You know, I thought you'd died."

"What?"

"I thought one of your big adventures had gotten you killed or something."

He reaches out to touch me. "Will—"

"You can ask Mum, she had to convince me that you'd all just moved away."

"Annabel or Mima?"

"What?"

"Which Mum managed to convince you?"

"Stop trying to be cute."

"Am I not succeeding?"

"No, you are, and it's annoying when I'm trying to be mad at you." I didn't want to look at him. I'd been so swept up, so taken along by all of it and I just wanted to curl up and hide. I should've stayed in my room. I should've kept my goddamn window shut despite how unbelievably hot it is. "You could have stayed in touch."

"So we vanished," he says, standing beside me, facing away from the pool. All of this suddenly feels like too much the night before my entire life is going to be thrown through a loop. "Mum needed an out, she packed a bag and we went and I never got to say goodbye. I hated that. I completely hated it."

"Yeah?"

"You were my best friend in the whole world," he says. "It hurt me to leave and not get to see you again. Then everything was overwhelming. Starting a new school, fitting in, settling in, and before I knew it…" he trails off.

"You forgot me."

"No—"

"Yes."

"No! I just lived the life I had," he says. "I thought about you still, I still missed you, I still looked back on all the fun we had when we were kids, of course I did, but I had to get on with it. I was eight." He sighs. "I found you online. Just like I found everyone else."

"You did?"

"Of course I did," he says. "You were the first person I looked for, the first person I found and I can't tell you how many messages and tweets I'd started to write but just couldn't send. It was one thing saying hello to everyone in here, but you were my best friend and I felt like I'd abandoned you. What could I have said?"

I smile. "'Hello' would've been a good start."

"Hello, William Darling."

"Please don't full-name me."

He grins that beautiful grin that just makes me weak. "Hello, William Michael Jonathan Darling."

"If anyone at Uni finds out my full name, it will be the end of me."

He takes hold of my hand. "I'm sorry, I'm sorry for all of it. I thought you would hate me, I thought I had already lost you."

A siren screams outside. I turn my head and see the blue lights flashing through the window. The party stalls so quickly I hardly have time to breathe. The music stops. People launch themselves from the pool and grab bags, rushing towards the fire exit.

Peter looks panicked.

"Grab the clothes!" he shouts.

I rush across and bundle them up in my arms, dashing after him and towards the fire exit that everyone is pouring out of. I see him in the crowd, a pasty white back disappearing into the distance. I give chase.

"Where are we going?"

Footsteps pound the pavement behind me. My chest heaves. My young heart threatening to give out.

"Second on the right," he says.

I follow him, darting down the second alleyway on the right, out into the train station car park. I still follow, straight across the road and into the parking garage. A hand reaches out and grabs me, pulling me to one side and into the stairwell.

"Up," he pants. "Up, go!"

I hurry up the stairs, my feet slapping against the wet floor. I don't want to think too hard about why it is wet, so I just keep on running. I can't hear anyone coming after us, I can't hear anyone else in here, but it doesn't stop me. I keep going until I reach the very top, until I see a bright red door, until I've slammed the door release hard and pushed through it, back out into the night and into the silence.

◖

I'd never seen the world like this before, my world. It sounds silly, but from up here, it all looks so small, so peaceful. My head may be a chaotic mess of contradictions and anxiety but up here, it's like they can float away.

Before I know it, I've dropped our clothes and walked to the edge, just taking in the town, the little twinkling lights of houses up on the hill.

"It's beautiful," I whisper into the night, like I'm telling it. *You're beautiful*, I should say. "I can't believe it's my last night here and I'm only just looking at it like this."

"How are you feeling about tomorrow?" Peter says. "Any better?"

"Worse."

"Why?"

I sigh. "I'm scared."

I turn to see him next to me. "Scared of what?"

"Of what will happen. Of what won't happen. Of what I could lose all over again. Of all of it. It makes me panic."

"Then don't think about it—"

"I have to—"

He takes hold of my shoulders and pulls me in close, kissing me hard on the lips. I feel myself melt into his arms, almost to a point where he is holding me up, but I catch myself and start to kiss him back, my arms snaking around his back and pulling his body closer.

This feels like flying.

We part, and even though he is barely half a metre away, I feel like I miss him.

"What are you thinking about now?"

"I was wondering how long it would be before you'd ruin the moment." I smile. "About three seconds."

"You're funny. Your housemates will love you."

His words drag me back to earth.

"I don't want to go."

"Try it," he says. "If you hate it, you can come home."

"I can do that?"

"You can do whatever you want."

He beckons me closer and leads me over to a patch of ground nearer the middle of the car park. He brings over our clothes. We get dressed. He lays his jacket down. We lay back, his hand in mine, my hand in his, and we watch the stars and clouds.

After a while, I notice the shift in the color of the sky. At some point I must've fallen asleep, because there's no way we could've just laid here talking all night. But the world is coming alive with sounds around us, breaking the magic we've found in our little patch of silence and I just want to press pause and live this moment for a few minutes longer.

A jolt of panic. "Wait, what time is it?"

He pulls his phone from his pocket. "Getting on for four. Why?"

"Shit." I get to my feet.

"What?"

"I'm supposed to be in the car at seven," I feel my body erupting in panicky goosebumps, my stomach flipping over at the thought of having to get in that car, of having to drive all the way to Uni and start my entire life all over again. Am I supposed to feel ready for this?

And then there's Peter. I'm going to have to part with Peter all over again, only this time, *I'm* the one that's vanishing. I look back at him and he has stood up too, casual, relaxed, so chilled out it makes me feel more anxious that I'm not as chilled as he is.

"You'll be fine," Peter says, closing the gap between us and leaning his forehead against mine. I close my eyes; breathing him in like it's the last time I'll ever see him. "I know you will."

"How do you know?"

He chuckles again, and even with my eyes closed I can see that electric smile on his face, the one that lifts those freckled cheeks and brightens up the whole universe. I'd missed that smile and I hadn't even realized it.

He reaches into my pocket and pulls out my phone, taking my thumb and placing it on the fingerprint sensor so it opens up. I can hear his fingers tapping against the screen. Then he locks it and puts in back in my pocket.

"You can call me if it gets too much," he says. "Any time. I'll answer that phone, I don't care where I am. I don't care what I'm doing."

"Will I ever see you again?" I open my eyes and find that he has done the same. I want to keep this moment. "I don't want to lose you again. Not now."

"Christmas?"

"What if you're not here again?"

"New Years?"

"Peter—"

"Fine," he says, reaching forward and taking hold of my hands, staring deep into my eyes. "One year from now, midnight, this rooftop. Whether I see you in between or not, I will be here." He leans in and kisses me softly on the lips. "I'll always be here, if you need me to be."

"I want you to be." I kiss him back, harder than he kissed me. I feel desperate, clawing at this moment to hold on.

"That settles it then." He checks his phone. "I reckon we've got an hour. Want to watch the world come alive?"

I want to tell him it already has, but it's so sweet-sounding I feel a little sick at the thought, so I just nod.

And we sit back on the concrete, right close to the edge, hand in hand, arm in arm, and we wait, watching the sun as it peeks over the hill, the coolness of the light hitting our faces. A new day. The beginning of something new, something bright. Maybe for both of us.

Dark Matters
by Tiffany Rose

A retelling of "Goldilocks and the Three Bears," this story adds a modern twist, as well as combining two of the best known versions of the tale.

When I was alive, my teachers said that most of the universe was dark matter. It was just a weird space fact at the time, but I remembered a few things from class. Scientists claim it doesn't interact normally, and it's only barely visible through indirect means. What they didn't teach in class was that no one could ever figure out what dark matter was until they became it. As it turns out, ghosts have similar properties, and my "once upon an undead" story wasn't going like I might have planned.

I stared down at the business card.

Kat T, Realtor
Going Above For Those Who Have Gone Beyond

How did other people read that line? For me, it meant I was now undead *and* looking for a home.

"I know this transition can be hard for people," the realtor said. I glanced up to her middle-aged corporeal form. "But ghosts who try to live the same life are often unable to move on. So, is it alright to call you Goldie?"

"Move on?' I repeated, ignoring the question.

"You know." She smiled and waved her hand towards the sky.

I was one thousand percent sure she didn't actually know, so I forced a smiled that quickly turned into a sigh. "This is the first house?"

"It is," she said cheerfully as she fiddled with the padlock over the door. This is what my life had become; figuring out where the hell to haunt, and thinking about ghost squatter's rights. "There is a couple who lives here now, but they'll be moved out within the week, so the place will be all yours. Until it sells, that is."

When I finally looked at the tiny home that was decorated to be "cute" instead of "cheap", I started to doubt this whole location. It would be a long walk out of the forest to get anywhere. While the woods and stars had that otherworldly feel, I didn't know if I wanted to throw my lot in with future tenants.

Everything was wood, in that artistic fire hazard style. It was a straight shot from "living room" to "kitchen" to a dead end of a loft bedroom that didn't have enough headroom for even a child to stand. Although I could likely phase through it if I focused, so maybe that could work.

"So, what do you think?" the realtor said, withholding any judgments she herself had about the place.

"Porridge."

She tilted her head, and I gestured to a one-person table which had a bowl of porridge sitting on it. I took a few more steps, which was the same as walking from one end of the house to the other, before turning back around.

"It's just—"

How did I sum up all my words, all of my discomfort about the quaint dread this place filled me with? That it made me want to scream *Is this all?*

"Too small."

"Yeah, you'd really have to make the whole forest your new home." Her expression pulled tighter, as if suggesting she agreed the whole time, then relaxed just as fast. "Let's try another."

The next house Kat showed me was even more than something else. I've heard some religions promised mansions when you died. Now, this medium-slash-realtor was offering me just that.

"This place has residents you'll have to share with, but it's unlikely you'll ever run into each other.

Unless, of course, you wanted to make the estate a tourist attraction," Kat joked.

"Right, of course." I laughed nervously. The large house reminded me of the desert. Both had a vastness that was uniform and unchanging. The inside continued in decadent fashion, filled with little more than empty space and echoes down distant halls.

This was too big. I didn't think I could ever take up enough space inside it, and it was a harsh reminder that I would never be able to grow into it. I tried to convince myself this is what every person hoped to achieve. Nations were built on the concept of wealth being the measure of success. Tombs were built as monuments and filled with riches gained over a lifetime.

"Thoughts on this one?" Kat asked, with a neutrality that must be trademarked by realtors.

"It's—" I stopped in front of a painting depicting a war. The battle didn't look familiar. Based on the white guy on the horse, and everyone else running away, I already sided with the persecuted. "Historical."

More than that, actually. It had an energy of its own. I reached my hand out, and the tips of my fingers felt pulled past my natural reach. They started to fade away before I ripped my hand back.

This place was already haunted by the past. If ghosts were dark matter, everyone who had passed this painting had also left the same weighted dark charge.

I glanced over to see if Kat caught any of it, but her focus was on an ornate vase. I took a step away from the painting and picked up a different vibe from the pottery. It held a coldness within the clay like a battery.

"I don't think this place is for me," I said softly. I hadn't meant to, but my voice didn't rise as much as a I thought it would.

"If I were undead, I think I'd pick here." Kat seemed to hum, or maybe there was a buzzing in my ears. "Well, let me at least show you the balcony before we leave."

As we walked, my feet struggled to make a sound against the carefully laid marble flooring. Had my steps been making noise before? I couldn't remember.

"Here we go." Kat drew open the drapes and flooded my vision with white.

I turned my head away, and had to fight for the life of me to get my eyes to readjust. I stepped back without even noticing until I was sitting in a large chair that may once have been for tea...if "sitting" was even the right word for what had happened. It seemed more like the chair had a gravity of its own.

The colors were off when I finally looked out at the large garden below the balcony. The sunlight washed the details away. I lifted my head like a royal who made all judgements with a discerning silence. There was one truth I now knew about this manor. Being myself here would be a struggle, fighting not to dissolve away like a shadow.

I didn't have Kat show me any more houses. She was good at her job, and being able to see me was rare enough. What else could you realistically want from someone? Still, I was resigned to wandering around and being a cold spot for strangers.

My time was filled with bumping around the planet and phasing through walls like I thought the world had a different floor plan than what physical reality suggested. There was noise, and light, and stuff everywhere, but none of it interacted directly with me. It didn't seem like I could be detected even by those who had the sight anymore.

Where I ended up was lost to me, but it had an interesting view. Standing in the immense drifts of snow was a house that stood out in that it didn't stand out. There was something uniquely beautiful about its average nature.

The walkway was shoveled, and a patch where a car normally sat was free of snow, making it clear someone lived here but wasn't currently home. I didn't see the harm in just checking out the place, so I went up to the front door and knocked. The sound alone made me smile. After just passing through life for a while, this door felt real. I don't know what I would have done if someone answered, but since they didn't, I focused on turning the handle and opening the door myself.

The living room was almost split between a cozy fireplace and a small den. One path lead upstairs, and another to a joint dining room and kitchen. There was a tool box on the table, and curiosity led me to open the lid. Not much inside, besides the basics: A hammer, interchangeable screwdriver, and measuring tape. Whatever needed repairing had already been fixed, or I hadn't seen it yet.

I ventured upstairs and found three rooms. The largest had a striped flag with shades of orange, yellow, and grey, with a paw print on the top left. It reminded me of the pink lipstick flag I used to have. Like the manor's collection, this too held an energy, but instead of a history that smothered, this had a cheerful pride.

Images of what sort of family lived here crossed my mind until I saw photos along a dresser. Their frames displayed heavy doors that opened out to showcase two men in suits holding each other's hands in the air. Their giant smiles parted wild and untamable beards.

There was another bedroom which shared a bathroom. Here the needed repair work was found, a patch of wall damaged by excess water from the shower. My fingers ran over the patch as bits of paint flaked off. This is what the toolkit had been pulled out to fix. It, too, made me smile. It showed that someone truly lived here.

The third room seemed to be mostly storage. There was a wooden rocking chair in one corner, and a few rolls of wrapping paper propped against boxes that hadn't been put away. It was a shrine to unfinished business and DIY possibilities. With a hum of approval, I decided to circle back to the welcoming rocking chair.

I woke up to the sound of mumbling. I didn't realize I had even fallen asleep until I noticed the now dim and near-sunless room. Sleeping certainly hadn't been something I meant to do, but the odd comfort here made it too easy to relax. The reprieve was soon ruined by voices downstairs.

"Halt, Evildoer!" a deep voice yelled. "Yee entered the house of bears who don't take kindly to intruders."

There was a definite pause between when I froze and when someone else spoke.

"Are you planning to scare off a home intruder with gay puns?"

The voices were closer now.

"Stop messing around."

That made three voices. I held my breath and hoped that was everyone. Just be invisible, I told myself. Just fade into the background, then sneak out.

"Wait," the same voice as last time went on. "I think Chris might be right, because I *know* I closed the tool box when we left."

Their footsteps made me flinch like they were the monsters creeping up the stairs. In reality, I knew I was the one haunting them. Jumping up from the chair, leaving it rocking in my wake, I stared at my hands and willed myself to be unseen.

When the door opened, we might have all yelped. The only clear thing was partially (and therefore uselessly) me. Then one of the trio of rugged-looking men swung his hand to hit the broad chest of another. "A ghost! I fucking told you I could see ghosts!"

"Unless we're all sharing a fever dream, I can see it, too."

I frowned, wondering if I could pull a full Halloween and flee. But the man quickly corrected himself.

"See her. Er, the ghost entity." In a hushed tone, he leaned towards the third guy and asked, "Do ghosts have gender?"

"I don't know," his voice spiked higher than I thought someone who looked like a lumberjack could. "This is the first time *I've* seen one."

"My name's Chris. Um, that's my husband, Richard, and that's our roommate George," he said, taking a quick glance at the other two, who were mostly in shock after their debate. His voice had a nervousness within it, but I think curiosity was winning out. "What's your name?"

My voice cracked at the simple sound I attempted to make, but I tried again. "My friends call me Goldie."

Chris took a step closer, and I might have taken one back if he had been intimidating as his size suggested. He was big, but seemed soft. Chris held his hand out, and I was surprised he didn't take it back in the time it took me to shake it.

"Ghosts can cast shadows?" Richard whispered from the door.

When I glanced up at him he flinched back. I didn't mean to scare him, I just didn't know I could do that. I pulled my hand back, I saw a shadow follow despite being translucent. "Whoa, what the hell."

"Why are you here?" Chris asked.

Oh. They didn't need to pull out a spirit board to learn the answer to that one. "I was looking for a place to be. I guess you could say I was thrown out of my place, and there was something about your house that caught my attention. It...feels loving."

I was trying to figure out how to better explain myself when an offer came that I never expected.

"Would you like to stay?" Chris asked, pausing for a half second at best. "As long as you don't do spooky shit around the house. Like, this right now needs to be max scariness."

"What?" George exclaimed. I think it was more of an involuntary sound than anything else.

Chris turned back, looking to Richard for help before sighing. "You were kicked out once, too. Come on. We can invite the ghost to stay."

George tilted his head as if conceding the point, a gesture that would have made him seem younger if not for the beard and well-worn leather jacket. I didn't know there was still a community that could sympathize with me. This trio might not be exactly like me, but they could become family all the same.

This home, with these three bears, was just right.

The Suns of Terre
by Will J. Fawley

*This spacefaring fairy tale is a version of "Prince Darling,"
which made its first known appearance in Andrew Lang's
<u>Blue Fairy Book</u>, published in 1889.*

> *If you treat the Corporation with love, the people
> will love you in return.*
> *But if you are cruel, the pain you inflict will be
> your own.*

I sit with Jote on the park bench that has become
our home. The park itself is really more of an alley,
hidden beneath the tangle of transportation wires which
connect the scrapers above. The walkways, the scrapers,

the bench, everything on the satellite is metallic, and that metal is rusted and chipping. A truck drives past. I grind my teeth and squeeze the extra hand that grows from my left elbow as the walkway beneath my feet rumbles.

"Relax," Jote says, "This place has been falling apart since before I was born, it'll last another day." I wrap my arms around him as he leans back against me. "Want any more?" he asks, holding a stick meat up to my mouth. I shake my head. Street food on the satellite is delicious, but greasy, and my stomach is still aching as it tries to digest the one I had for breakfast.

Jote laughs, understanding my refusal without an explanation.

"Sorry," I say, feeling rude for refusing satellite food. He must think I'm such a snob.

He's looking up at the blue glow of Terre in the sky, the capital planet of the Terren Corporation of Worlds—the corporation I'm supposed to be in charge of now. "It's fine," he says.

"I just wish it was easier." The words are strange in my mouth. I dcn't have much practice talking out loud.

"I was going to leave soon anyway. It doesn't matter if they kicked me out."

"You were going to leave?" I ask, realizing we're not talking about the same thing.

"Yeah, I had to leave my keepers sometime."

"Not just because of me?" My extra hand twitches.

"It wasn't because of you."

"Yes it was."

"Okay, it was a little bit you," Jote says, "but not for the reason you think. They just wanted me gone, and catching us gave them the excuse they were looking for." I shrug and he keeps talking. "Look, you don't have to feel guilty. I had nothing to lose—you on the other hand…"

"It's not losing. I'm gaining you."

We kiss and I feel a little nauseous when I taste the grease of the stick meat on his lips. I mean it, though. I am prepared to give up Terre, my heirship, everything. And it's not a totally selfless decision—if I stay here on the satellite, I never have to become president.

"It's true what they say about pretty guys…" Jote says as he pulls away and studies my face.

"They're weak." I say, completing the satellite saying.

Jote blinks but his third eye stays open, as it always does since it doesn't have an eyelid. "Your words, not mine," he chuckles. "I was going to say, they're all Terrens."

We laugh together. I realize it's the first time I've let myself laugh since my father died.

A Terre security officer walks toward us. He couldn't make me go back, but I really don't feel like defending my actions right now, so I lift my hood to cover my ring.

When Terren children are born, a metal ring is fused to the top of our craniums. The ring lets us control and alter our genetic makeup. Hair usually grows over the ring quickly because they're made of a thin wire, but with the extra features my father added to mine, it bulges even through my bushy mutant hair. I may as well be projecting a script from my head that says "Darl of Terre here."

"Sir," the officer says, nodding his perfect head at me as he passes. Jote and I giggle at the absurdity of me in my true form, the high-society mutant.

Jote pushes the hood back and runs his fingers through the hair around my ring. "You're beautiful like this," he says. He studies my blotchy, dark arm against his own pale skin that's mottled with boils and birthmarks the color of mine. It's like looking through holes in him and seeing myself.

He pulls me in for a kiss, but I break free from the embrace. The ground is vibrating and I'm wondering if this will be the shake that finally tears the fake moon from the sky, but it's just the heavy footsteps of a thug approaching.

She stops when she reaches us, her tall frame sliding between the narrow shadows of the scrapers. Her eyes are vertical slits in her green face, but it's her noses that really makes you stare. She's got two of them and they're fused together like tilting scrapers.

"Evening, lover boys," the thug barks. She also has an extra row of bottom teeth that poke out from her deformed lips at odd angles so she can't quite close her mouth. Her eyes stare through us, a clear sign she's buzzed on street slap.

"We're not interested," I say. This is my standard greeting on the satellite. Whether they're interested in buying or selling, drugs or hacked rings, it covers all the bases.

I reach up to make sure my hair is covering the ring, but the thug must catch a glimpse of it.

"What's this?" she asks, looking at my bulky ring, which gives me away. "I'd heard the heir ran away after his daddy died. Most of us would give anything for a fraction of his good fortune, but even when the universe was handed to him on a golden platter, he swatted the opportunity away like a swarm of degonflies." Her teeth gnash as she laughs.

My father loved the degonflies, their long abdomens glowing with bioluminescencet light. In those final days when he could do nothing else, Shara and I sat at his bedside and the three of us watched the saffa trees in the courtyard become galaxies as the degonflies lit up like uncountable stars.

Rage quickly masks the memories, and I jump from the bench to attack the thug. My misshapen left leg buckles under me, which slows me down enough for Jote to pull me back onto the bench. I'm trying to breathe rhythmically, the way my tutor Shara trained me to block the rage. In through the nose, out through the mouth. But the anger only weakens. It never dies.

"Come on, let's go," Jote says. I nod. I get enough shit back home. Some of my earliest memories are of so-called perfect Terrens spitting at me and calling me names—Spoiled Brat, Pampered Pansy, Darling Prince. The last one hurt the most because it was the nickname my father gave me, twisted into a barbed insult.

The thug continues, "I never thought someone as far above us as the heir to the Corporation would be caught dead on this junk heap."

"Look, we're really not interested," Jote says, tightening his grip on my good arm.

"Wasting your time with satellite trash," the thug slurs at me as she nods her head toward Jote. I'm used to being mocked—being the better man, as Shara would say—but all the breathing in the world can't calm me when the thug goes after Jote.

"Filthy shit," I say, distracting the thug while I send a ring notification to the security officer nearby. "Even with two noses, you can't figure out you need a bath."

The mutant growls and pauses as if to reply, but then she turns to walk away.

"Arrest this thug," I say to the officer. My scalp begins to crawl with electricity.

"But sir, she hasn't done anything to warrant arrest. I can't…"

"I said arrest her!" I shout. The ring sends a jolt through my skeleton and the street around me blurs.

Through the haze, I see my father. In this memory I am a child and he is walking beside me in the headquarters courtyard that blurs in the heat of Terre's twin suns. Rows of perfectly manicured saffa trees line the courtyard's paths, which are coated in the pastel powder that falls from the trees' seed pods.

"My only wish for you, son," my father says, "is that you be a good man. To help you, I've had your ring equipped with a feature that will correct you when you misbehave. You must always be a good boy. Can you do that for me?"

I nod. He smiles and then begins to waver in the heat rays. A degonfly swirls up toward the satellite.

"Sir," the security officer says, supporting me as I slump to the side, "are you alright?"

"Yes, I'm fine," I say as Jote helps me up. The thug is being led away in light cuffs and soon she disappears between the shadows of the doomed buildings.

I take a deep breath, rust and oil coating my throat as I finally accept that while I will never be as good as my father wanted me to be, I can't let that stop me from becoming president, from having the power to protect people like Jote, and myself. I'm done acting out Shara's martyr fantasies.

I kiss Jote as I ring Shara.

☾

A feed of the headquarters courtyard on Terre projects from the device implanted in my skull, and I find myself longing for my perfect Terren form—two perfect arms and two perfect legs, silky black hair covering my ring, my skin smooth and dark. A pair of degonflies float by on the feed, one chasing the other around a guard's head. He swats at them, but they are too quick.

The saffa trees in the garden are mostly projections now—projections of projections, their true forms lost like everything on Terre. It started because we valued beauty above truth, but now we make fake things out of necessity because the planet is reverting back to the desert world it once was—rejecting the terraforming that sought to perfect its image the way the rings perfect ours. In the end, the joke's on us, because the chemical byproducts of the blasting and reshaping we did to beautify the planet are what mutated us into the forms we now use our rings to hide.

A door slams and Shara's tall frame comes huffing into view in the courtyard feed. It's kind of hilarious how angry she is all the time, when you consider she spends hours on end training me in the boring arts of meditation and pacifism. She's the only Terren I know who is grumpy enough to override their good looks.

I'm expecting her to scold me for taking so long to accept my responsibility, but when she ringspeaks, she says, "You can't just throw a mutant in jail because it pleases you."

"Why not?"

"Why not?" I can hear the hesitance in her voice as she searches for words amidst her frustration. "Because you are the heir and you must uphold your father's good name, for one. Have I not taught you anything?"

"The thug insulted Jote," I say, picturing him homeless and alone on our park bench as the scrapers crumble around him.

"Yes, I heard. She shouldn't have been so foolish, but that is no reason to arrest her. It was a mess getting her released. More importantly, you need to realize your actions have consequences, Darl. It's how we act in moments like these that define who we are as Terrens, and in your case, as the soon-to-be president. And who knows. Though the thug's words were out of place, maybe they are worth considering?"

"I can't believe you're taking her side," I say, instinctively grabbing for my extra hand. "I'm sick of giving up my own happiness for the sake of the Corporation, for a figurehead position that requires me to live by some imaginary moral code." An electric storm gathers in my skull.

"Darl, with your father…with him not here anymore, you have to think about how your actions reflect on the Corporation."

"I'm tired of pretending to be better than human. I'm not. None of us are. We're all mutants under the pretty ring technology. The only difference is that some of us can afford to hide our ugly sides."

"I know it's hard to accept, but it's time to face reality. Jote was a fine suitor, but we both know he's not a fit co-president."

"Because he's a mutant."

"It's more complicated than that."

"I'm done with your mindgames. I'm coming back to Terre," I say as I summon a shuttle.

The degonflies are now locked together on a saffa leaf, and I can't tell if they're loving or fighting.

My ring beeps. "What was that?" I ask, studying Shara's scowl for an answer as the shuttle pulls up.

"You must be protected from yourself."

"What are you talking about?" I knock on the shuttle's windows because the doors aren't opening.

"Your transit permissions have been revoked. It's for your own good."

"I am the president," I growl through the lightning that strikes me harder with each quickening beat of my pulse. "All my life I've been mocked and teased for being the 'Darling Prince,' the good boy who turns the other cheek for any common thug." I remember all the times I was mocked, laughed at, and rejected, the reason I went to the satellite that first time—to escape from the pressure of being the president's son. "That ends now."

"You're not the president yet." Shara shakes her head, not realizing that I'm serious. I'm done being hurt, and I'll do what I have to to take care of myself and Jote. Who else do I have?

"Arrest her!" I command the courtyard security officer.

Shara's eyes go wide with shock and she opens her mouth, but the know-it-all is at a loss for words. The security officer gives me a condescending pity-smile as the pain from the ring's jolt zaps down my spine.

The world melts into a sea of colors that drown me until I become lost in them. From inside, they look different. They twist out of themselves. They become words. *You have abused your power for your own gain, Darl,* they say in my father's voice. *You are no longer worthy of Terre.* My tongue is salty with swallowed tears and the pain blasts me again, tearing through every cell of my body. ***Your genetic alteration powers have been suspended.***

I feel something tugging me as the colors come back. The feed shuts off and the projected courtyard disappears, leaving me in the cold reality of the decaying satellite. I bang on the shuttle door again, and it drives away.

"Wait, come back! You can't leave me. I'm..." What's the point? Everyone has their own opinions of what I should be, but no one cares who I really am.

(

As Jote and I stand in line at a stick meat cart, the satellite groans, buckling under its own weight. Jote laughs at me when I tense up, and I force myself to take a stomach breath and accept that the decay is something I'll have to get used to. While Jote studies the three items on the menu, I look up through the haze at the blur of Terre in the sky and wonder how this is supposed to be a punishment. So what if my ring privileges are gone? What's wrong with being stuck as myself?

Jote buys one of each type of stick: mystery meat one, two, and three. Apparently they were all too good to pass up. He hands me one and I take a bite, savoring the greasy meat. Maybe I can get used to this place.

I'm still chewing through the gristle of my first stick when Jote tosses his garbage and starts on a second. He looks up at me. "Good, right?"

I nod. He looks inside me the way he does, with all his eyes opening me up, and I sigh because I know he sees what I'm thinking, but I still have to say it out loud because he doesn't have a ring. "I just can't stop thinking about the thug Shara released. It's so unfair."

"So what, you wanna go find her?"

"What? No." I take another bite and wipe my greasy lips on my sleeve. "I mean, I don't think so. Do I?"

"I know that look, the way you stare up at Terre when something's bothering you."

"What do I do if I find her?"

"Whatever you want, you're the President of the Great Corporation of Terren Worlds," he says, attempting a Terren accent.

"Not yet."

"But you *will* be. Let's go find that thug."

To get back to the park, we take a shortcut through a forest of weeds that grows out of the rust-lined cracks in the walkway. The ring feels weightless on my head as we walk, and now that it's useless, I forget that it's there.

"It's okay," Jote says as we hack through the weeds.

"What is?"

"I'm not mad at you for wanting to go back. You're sick of running. I know what that's like."

I nod, but I'm not listening because everything seems to be tilted at an odd angle. I ask Jote if he notices it, but he says I'm still having culture shock since everything back on Terre is perfectly aligned. Here the scrapers slant, and there are no degonflies. I massage my extra hand until the pressure hurts.

I'm thinking about the courtyard and the artificial beauty of Terre when a gust of wind blows by and seems to say my name. But it's not the wind, it's a group of thugs following us.

"You're nothing now, Prince Darling," says the female thug I had arrested.

"Who said I wanted to be anything?"

"Smartass," she says through all those clacking teeth.

My first instinct is to transform back into Terren form—for power, for control—but I realize that's not me anymore. I take a step toward the thug, and suddenly the metal beneath our feet groans and shakes.

I give in to the panic as the shaking gets worse. A nearby scraper tumbles, and mutants run from the collapsing building. The scene reminds me of an ancient painting of Hell my father told me about—misshapen people, screaming and running through fire.

I grab onto Jote to keep from falling. The thug claws at the ground and starts sliding downward as the satellite tilts and the metal sheets crack apart at their rusted seams. Jote grabs onto a pole with his free hand, but our fingers slip apart and I slide toward the thug.

As the satellite shakes again, the thug slides down toward an opening in the sidewalk. She claws wildly at the ground as she slides against the metal and falls into the crack, just managing to grab the edge of the ground to keep from falling. She thrashes her legs and tries to pull herself back up, but instead she falls farther into the hole.

"Darl!" Jote shouts as he reaches out to me, but he is too far and I am slipping away. My shirt catches on a rusted patch of walkway and slides up to my chest. The metal scrapes my stomach. My abdomen feels wet and burns with something stronger than fire, but all I can think about is the zap of my ring and how I want nothing more than to watch the thug slide down and be crushed by the gears that make the satellite spin around Terre. The shuddering stops, but the thug is still hanging from the edge of the sidewalk when something strange comes over me.

I realize that the bitter anger I've been carrying is just a fear of the zap, a pain I'd resigned myself to. Now that the ring is off, I'm free to make my own decisions—help the thug, or watch her fall to her death. With the anger gone, I don't want to watch anyone die. I crawl toward the crack and help the thug back up onto the sidewalk.

"Thank you, sir," she says between breaths. When she's breathing normally again, she pulls her hair back to reveal a ring. Then her mutations melt into her flesh as she becomes a perfect Terren, an oddity among the mutants who rush to rescue the casualties of the shake.

"What the hell?" I ask as her form bleeds back into that of Shara. For some reason, I hug her, and she smiles, maybe for the first time since my father died.

"I'm sorry for the deception," Shara says as I gain control of my emotions and pull away, "but it was all part of your father's plan."

"His plan?" I ask, wondering how a man as kind and honorable as my father could have planned the zap that caused such pain and anger. I have to believe he didn't, that it was just a side effect.

"His plan to ensure that you were fit to rule Terre. You will find that your ring is operational again."

A warmth echoes from my ring, through my skull, and vibrates throughout my body, not in a painful way, but in a way that makes me think my heartbeat has been altered.

Jote takes my hand and I squeeze our fingers together.

I want to believe Shara now, but I have to wonder if this is for real or just some sick punchline to the rest of her training. I decide to give *her* a test. "Okay, so say I did go back to Terre and become president now. What happens to Jote and everybody on the satellite?"

"The very act of your becoming president will send a message to the entire Corporation that satelliters and Terrens revolve around the same suns."

I don't know if she passes the test or not. Her answer sounds good, but how can I just go back to Terre after all this? If there's one thing the ring has taught me, it's that nothing and no one can tell you which choice is right or wrong. All I can do is trust myself to make the decisions that are best for the Corporation. And if accepting the presidency means equality between the people of Terre and the satellite, then that's the choice I have to make.

"What are you waiting for?" Shara asks. "Go ahead and change back."

Jote takes my hand, and I look into his eyes—my mutant form is reflected in all three of them, and I finally see myself the way he does. "There's no going back," I say. "This is me."

(

Jote, Shara, and I fly back to Terre together for what could only be described as my coronation. Thousands of people crowd together in the manicured streets of the capital city, mutants and ringers side by side in front of the headquarters. The asymmetrical buildings look less stable than the scrapers on the satellite, and I massage my extra hand even though I know the structures are mostly illusion.

Jote is sweating and I take his hand in my free one. "This planet is too hot," he says.

"You sure it's the planet?" I say. "Because I think it's just you." I kiss him above his third eye. He laughs nervously and pushes my face away.

"I don't know if I can do this." Jote's adorable lidless eye dilates.

"You don't have to."

"I know. But I need to." He smiles through the sweat. "I mean I want to."

"We're projecting," Shara says through ringspeak. In her face is a gentleness I'd almost forgotten was possible.

I look up to the projection platform where likenesses of Jote and I stand, tall as scrapers towering over the crowd, our huge mutant deformities proudly on display.

Cheers erupt through the streets below, and Jote grips my hand as a single voice echoes from the crowd in ringspeak, "Mutant scum! You'll never…" Someone knocks the elitist to the ground and the cheers get louder.

"Citizens of Terre," Shara begins, her voice booming through the skies as she speaks aloud so everyone can hear, even the ringless mutants. "For too long we have been divided. But today we are reminded that our planet's satellite is just that, *our* satellite. It belongs to this planet, and to the Corporation—all of us do. It is with heavy hearts that we remember those lost in the tragedy of the shake, but crews are already at work rebuilding a safer satellite, so it is with hope that we look toward the future. How fitting it is for us to recognize today, a new dawn, a union of everything we are." More cheers.

"I now present the first mutants to rule our Great Terren Corporation of Worlds, your new co-presidents, Darl and Jote of Terre!"

Shara leans over me and attaches the full-access ring upgrade to my old one, and then she attaches Jote's as well—we can become anything. Standing next to Shara, I recognize in her smile, her smile that was lost to me, a piece of my father I never thought I would know again.

"Today is not just about Jote and I, it is about all of us," I say aloud as I look up at the projection of my giant, imperfect body with its deformed limbs and blotchy skin. "My father was a great leader, but he made mistakes," I continue, the echo of the ring's zap sending shivers through all my limbs. "I can't promise I'll be perfect, but I will learn from his mistakes as I learn from my own. One of my father's biggest mistakes was introducing these rings. They are a veil over the reality of our planet and the true beauty of our people. So I ask you to turn your genetic alteration features off. We will no longer ignore the problems that face us, but will tackle them head on—together. No matter our appearance, we are all Terrens. Whether we live on the satellite, here on the capital planet, or any world of the Corporation, we are *all* Terrens."

A blip goes through the crowd as ringers disable their genetic modifications in solidarity, reverting to mutant form. They look around throughout the crowd, unsure at first, not recognizing their own natural bodies. A cry erupts from the mass of people, "We are all Terrens!" The crowd begins chanting the mantra together. The voices from the sea of natural, perfect creatures grows louder until they become a high-pitched buzz, which melts into the sound of my ring transmitting a message notification through my skull.

Shouts echo from a cluster of people who haven't turned their genetic modification features off. My ring buzzes again. More shouts. The remaining ringers are beating a mutant and won't let him up.

"It can't be like this," I say as Jote leads me away from the projector. "It can't. Not anymore." My ring keeps buzzing.

"Come on," Jote says. "Change doesn't come easy, but this is only the beginning. You are changing the world, and I'm right here beside you. Together we will unify all Terrens."

My ring is buzzing incessantly now. I can't ignore it any longer. I project once more and wave to the crowd with all of my hands before excusing myself into the courtyard for privacy. The recorded message begins.

"My Darling Prince," my father's voice says, *"You must know that I love you dearly and that I never doubted your judgment for a moment. I needed you to be ready to take over my role when the time came. Shara was to step in at the end, to push you to your limits and give you one final lesson that would allow you to prove to yourself that you were ready. By now I'm sure you have discovered that you are.*

The enhancement to your ring was not meant to control or test you, but to prepare you for the decisions you will have to make as president, to challenge you and make you better than your former self. I always knew you would become the man you are now, the leader our corporation needs."

The suns are setting now, their falling light distorting the beauty of the projected saffa trees and illuminating the silhouette of the satellite in the sky. Jote comes out to join me in the courtyard. He wraps an arm around my waist, and together we look up at the sky of our corporation as a degonfly rises into the disappearing light.

About the Authors

Laure Nepenthes is an aspiring writer from the south of France. They enjoy telling stories, counting the stars at night, and making sure that their cats are the one and only rulers of the neighbourhood. This is their first published work of original fiction.

Rachel Sharp is an author and freelance editor living in New York City. She likes gardening and ukuleles. She is currently working on her fourth novel, <u>An Epitaph for Everything Else</u>. Follow on Twitter @WrrrdNrrrdGrrrl, or find her at wrrrdnrrrdgrrrl.com

Amy Michelle is a legal assistant living in North Carolina. When she's not working, writing, or taking care of her three cats, she enjoys throwing her paycheck at recreating intricate costumes with cosplay. Follow her on Tumblr at geminibadgerbooks.tumblr.com or Twitter @GeminiDragonAM

Bec McKenzie is the Creative Director of Alt-Tabby, an indie game studio, and lives in North Carolina. She has cerebral palsy, a wry sense of humor, and two cats that demanded a mention somewhere. Her writing on video games can be found scattered like breadcrumbs around the internet, and more fiction is in the works. Follow her on Twitter @KittenCrit.

Saffyre Falkenberg is a graduate student from Texas pursuing her MA in English and Women & Gender Studies. She currently works as the managing editor of the *descant* and is writing her first young adult fantasy novel. Baking cookies, drinking coffee, and playing *Dragon Ag*e are some of her favorite pastimes. When she's not writing or reading, she's probably chasing her three cats around. Follow on Twitter @thebooksapphire or find her online at thebooksapphire.wordpress.com.

Moira C. O'Dell is the one responsible for rearranging all the supermarket shelves once you've gotten used to where everything is. She studied vocal music and creative writing at Alderson-Broaddus University and is currently working on her own compilation of original and adapted fairy tales featuring LGBT+ characters. She shares her West Virginia home with her mother, sister, and three african hedgehogs. Visit her on Tumblr at moriawrites.tumblr.com.

Minerva Cerridwen is a pharmacist from Belgium who has always loved writing fiction. She enjoys baking and calligraphy. Since 2013 she has been writing for paranatellonta.tumblr.com and she is currently working on her first science fiction novel. Find her on Twitter @minerva_cerr.

Dominique Cyprès is a beleaguered stock clerk from Massachusetts. They enjoy stereo photography and red curry. They are currently working on a novel and a collection of poetry to follow up on their first book, <u>Dogs</u>

from your childhood & other unrealities. Follow them on Twitter or Instagram @lunasspecto.

Kassi Khaos is a student trying to remain somewhat sane while surviving endless projects and papers. She lives in Ohio, where the two seasons are winter and construction. She writes until she writes herself out, usually singing show tunes all the while. She's the author of at least one and a half good fanfictions; The rest shall not be mentioned.

Elspeth Willems is a university student from Florida. She enjoys gloomy days, art projects, and new books. This is her first published work of fiction, and she is currently working on a novel fueled by her love of fantasy and romance. You can find her on Twitter @ElspethWillems.

Will Shughart is a writer living in the mountains of Utah. He likes old maps, forgotten classics, and unusual waffle recipes. He is currently working on his first novel. Follow him on Twitter @willshughart.

Emmy Clarke is a children's author living in the north of the UK. She enjoys collecting funky lookin' twigs, petting strange cats, and eating unhealthy amounts of pasta. So far, she has published one book for under tens, Luch & Friends. Follow her on Twitter @EmmyAClarke, Instagram @starmaid, or check out her website emmyclarkeblog.wordpress.com.

George Lester grew up in Essex but now lives in London, where he pretends to be a grown up on a daily basis. When he isn't writing, you would find him hanging out with his better half, performing with a local Musical Theatre group, or making videos on YouTube. He is represented by Sam Copeland at RCW and is currently working on his first novel. You can follow him on Twitter (and in most other places) @TheGeorgeLester, or on YouTube at youtube.com/GesterG91

Tiffany Rose is a full-time writer and activist from Las Vegas. She spends her free time looking for plot bunnies and waiting for her Starfleet uniform to arrive. Her debut novel, <u>Hello World,</u> comes out this Winter. For a dose of science fiction now, check out her video game inspired Bone Diggers free on Wattpad. Follow her personal Twitter @FromPawnToQueen, or, for book only tweets, check out @ArtOverChaos.

Will J. Fawley is a proposal writer by day and a fiction writer by night. He lives in Winnipeg, Canada, where he enjoys playing video games in winter and skateboarding in July. His short queer speculative fiction has appeared or is forthcoming in *The Northern Virginia Review*, *Expanded Horizons*, and *Another Place*. Follow him on Twitter @willjfawley or find him at willjfawley.com

Acknowledgments

The editor's thanks go out to Zora Parker, who always supports my big ideas and makes them seem truly doable. Thanks for getting this project off the ground.

To Rachel Sharp, the fairy godmother of this collection. This book would not exist without her editorial magic in the time of greatest need.

To over a dozen writers featured in this collection, for your words, faith, and the reminder of the "happily ever afters" this community can create.

To everyone who submitted stories and believed that a collection like this should exist.

And to you, the reader, for bringing new life to these stories by touching them with your own heart.

- Tiffany Rose

Made in the USA
Lexington, KY
26 October 2016